Praise for **bumped**

"BUMPED is brilliant, innovative, and slightly terrifying. Megan McCafferty delivers!"
—Carolyn Mackler, author of the Printz Honor Book THE EARTH, MY BUTT, AND OTHER BIG ROUND THINGS and coauthor of THE FUTURE OF US

"Megan McCafferty has conceived a hilarious, touching, truly original novel, told in her trademark, spot-on voice. Readers of every age will delight in this new arrival."
—Rachel Cohn, bestselling author of NICK & NORAH'S INFINITE PLAYLIST

"BUMPED has it all—a fascinating yet frighteningly believable world, seamless world-building, great humor, and sophisticated wordplay. The characters are sexy and complicated in the best ways. The book will start many a discussion and, alas, raise more than a few eyebrows. I suspect the mothers will like it just as much as the da~~ ~~ers. BUMPED is the 'breediest' novel of the year."
                    —Gabrielle Zevin

"McCafferty proves that d~~...~~ ~~...~~-y to be provocative."   ~~...~~s Weekly

"BUMPED has plenty to say abou~~...~~ ~~...~~productive rights and girls' place in society."   —ALA Booklist

"An adventure of clashing cultures, challenged beliefs, and, yes, mistaken identity." —*Bitch* magazine

"BUMPED is wonderfully original, with an extremely well thought-out dystopian society, the details of which the reader deduces through context and dialogue, rather than via a dull prologue. The protagonists begin as manifestations of two extreme political points, but morph into stunningly human portrayals of conflict and a search for autonomy. McCafferty's future echoes just enough of current events to seem chillingly possible." —*Romantic Times*

bumped

MEGAN McCAFFERTY

Balzer + Bray
An Imprint of HarperCollins*Publishers*

Balzer + Bray is an imprint of HarperCollins Publishers.

Bumped
Copyright © 2011 by Megan McCafferty
All rights reserved. Printed in the United States of America.
No part of this book may be used or reproduced in any manner whatsoever
without written permission except in the case of brief quotations embodied in
critical articles and reviews. For information address HarperCollins Children's
Books, a division of HarperCollins Publishers, 10 East 53rd Street, New York,
NY 10022.
www.epicreads.com

Library of Congress Cataloging-in-Publication Data
McCafferty, Megan.
Bumped / Megan McCafferty. — 1st ed.
    p. cm.
Summary: In New Jersey in 2036, when teen girls are expected to become
fanatically religious wives and mothers or high-priced Surrogettes for couples
made infertile by a widespread virus, sixteen-year-old identical twins Melody
and Harmony find in each other the courage to believe they have choices.
ISBN 978-0-06-196275-2
[1. Pregnancy—Fiction. 2. Infertility—Fiction. 3. Twins—Fiction. 4. Sisters—
Fiction. 5. Choice—Fiction. 6. Virus diseases—Fiction.] I. Title.
PZ7.M47833742Bum 2011   2010030704
[Fic]—dc22   CIP
                                                                    AC

Typography by Jennifer Rozbruch
12 13 14 15 16   CG/RRDH   10 9 8 7 6 5 4 3 2 1
                              ❖
First paperback edition, 2012

For Caitlyn, Carly, Cailey, and Zoë—
when you're old enough

FIRST

The United States of America once ranked above all industrialized nations in the realm of teen pregnancy. We were the undisputed queens of precocious procreation! We were number one before, and we can be number one again!
—President's State of the Union Address

melody
harmony

I'M SIXTEEN. PREGNANT. AND THE MOST IMPORTANT PERSON on the planet.

According to the Babiez R U ad, anyway.

"You're knocked up," sings the girlie chorus. *"Ready to pop. Due to drop."* The sixty-second jingle loops continuously in the dressing room.

I check the MiNet to make sure no one I know is shopping in this wing of the Meadowlands Mallplex. Most of my friends are still in bed sleeping off last night's Tocin hangovers. I'm safe.

"Do the deed. Born to breed."

Free from neggy eyes, I could act just like the fat and happy models in the commercials. I could shout, I could shimmy, I could show off every pound of my, um, *abundant awesomeness.* Such gushing doesn't come as naturally to me as it does to other girls. I have to work harder at it, the way my friends struggle to solve calculus equations that are easy for me. Preparing to pregg is a full-time job with no days off—but I don't have a choice. Not when there's so much at stake.

Rubbing my spectacularly distended belly, I want to try out an expression just to hear how it sounds coming out of my mouth.

"I'm . . ."

Egging. Preggiiing . . .

"Fertilicious?"

My whole body sags under the weight of my sigh. I'm supposed to *own* my pregnancy because my *extra sixty is oh so sexy,* but I'd die of embarrassment if anyone I know caught me striking poses like this—especially Zen. So I guess it's a good thing that my best friend has made no effort to see me lately.

"Went forth and multiplied. Fightin' the omnicide . . ."

I check once more for anyone I know, then blind my MiNet with a blink-left-right-left-wink-double-blink. The song is wrapping up—*"You're the most important person on the plaaaanet. . . . Babiez R U!"*—when I'm startled out of my reverie by the sound of my own voice.

"Well!"

I jump.

I've been so focused on my own expectant spectacle, I forgot that I'm not alone in the dressing room. Standing

2

directly behind me is Harmony. Until a few weeks ago, we had never spoken. And until a few hours ago, we had never met in person.

She's my identical twin.

harmony
melody

I LOVE THE MEADOWLANDS MALLPLEX!

It's fast and loud and bright and buzzing with temptation but that's why I love it. I love it because there's no better place for me to do the work I was born to do: to spread the Word. Everyone in Goodside is already on message, but here there's an endless supply of sinners going down the wrong path. It's dizzying trying to decide who to witness to first. Or rather, next. After Melody.

I'm here because I lost my best veil. It was so silly, really. I didn't tell Melody the whole story because I was afraid she'd laugh at me, or compare me to a happy puppy as Angel did after she calmed down when she saw that my stunt on the bridge hadn't done anyone any harm.

Angel is the driver I called to take me to Otherside. I

don't know if that's her name or not, but I like to think that it is. I had seen the billboard on Route 381 a few months ago, the last time it was my turn to leave Goodside to sell my fruit preserves at the Fayatte County Farmers' Market.

Angel Cab Company

1-800-GOD-TRIP

The LORD will watch over your coming and going.

Psalm 121

A pair of wings sprouted from the shoulders of the *A* in "Angel." It wasn't difficult to commit the ad to memory, though I'm not sure why I did. At the time, I didn't know about Melody and had nowhere else to go.

Angel isn't in the Church but she does have God, which is as blessed as you can get in Otherside. She pulled up promptly at four a.m. and was full of the spirit despite the short notice, early hour, and her advanced age. Her white hair was cropped like a newly shorn lamb's, her skin the warm brown of a biscuit ready to be taken out of the oven. With her crinkling eyes and ready smile, I trusted her immediately. Even more so when she asked, "Are you ready to let go and let God?"

I liked that. It reminded me that I wasn't leaving my faith behind, it's always here with me.

"I am!" I said, buckling myself into the backseat.

If paying someone to take me from Goodside to

Princeton sounds indulgent, you're right. But I don't know how to drive and have no access to mass transit maps and schedules and once I decided to leave I really didn't have any time to waste on figuring it all out. I made the right choice because Angel said it would've taken me sixteen hours and four transfers (bus, bus, train, train, shuttle bus) to travel three hundred miles. I might have made it past the Goodside gates, but probably not much farther than that before someone took notice of the Church girl traveling all by herself. Angel Cab traveled the same distance in just over three. I was halfway to Princeton before first light, and arrived on my sister's doorstep in time for a breakfast prayer! The one-way fare cost all the money I had in the world, but that's just one of many worries I'm choosing not to bother myself with right now.

I've taken missionary trips to other mallplexes with my prayerclique, but I've always had a chaperone and traveled on the Church bus. I suppose I could have asked Melody to MiBuy me a veil—it isn't *quite* as important to try them on as I led her to believe—but I want to make the most of my time with her. I want to go out and see the world beyond Goodside. I want to reach as many people as possible. If I serve well, this could be a life-changing experience for both of us.

It has to be.

When Melody suggested we browse at Babiez R U, I got nervous. I knew it wasn't a place of righteousness. Stores like this make a mockery out of Heaven's greatest gifts and my housesisters testify all the time about how bad company ruins good habits, which is why I'm so lucky to have them in my life. But I have complete faith in my faith. There's no reason to be afraid of anything I see here.

I pray that by joining Melody in this store, we will finally twinbond. It's been a month since our miraculous reunion and she has yet to call me sister. In fact, she has yet to say much to me at all, unless I ask her directly. Melody has been open about herself but uncurious about me, answering ten times the number of questions that she has asked, a tally that stands at three: "What are you doing here?"; "Why didn't you tell me you were coming?"; and "I don't think you'll need another veil while you're here but if it's that important to you then I guess we can go to the Mallplex, okay?"

Despite her reticence, just standing next to my sister is as exhilarating as cruising across the Benjamin Franklin Bridge, over the Delaware River, the cab taking me out of one state and into the next just as the sun crowned the horizon. . . .

That's how I lost my best veil.

I longed to merge with this glorious landscape! I longed to unite with the majestic skyline! I longed to revel in His goodness at a hundred miles per hour. I lowered the window and stuck out my head, and shouted out.

"Hallllleeeeeellllluuuuuujaaaaaaaaaaaah!"

Angel screamed, swerved, screeched the breaks, and screamed some more. We were blessed that there aren't too many cars on the road at sunrise.

Once I was safe back inside the car, she prayed about my recklessness before saying she was surprised to see such behavior out of a Church girl like me.

"You don't need to return to His kingdom *right now*, do you, love?"

She was right. I didn't need to meet my Maker today. Especially after I'd gone through so much trouble to get here.

I'll never forget the sight of my veil in the split seconds after it freed itself from my tangled hair, soaring, up, up, upward, closer to Heaven, a dazzling flash of white against the pink and blue sky.

melody
harmony

I CAN'T GET A CLEAR LOOK AT HARMONY'S FACE. IT'S THAT veil.

I tried to talk her out of wearing it in public but she's not having it. In her defense, I guess it makes sense because why would she wear her veil in *private*? Harmony managed to lose her "best" veil during the ride to my house—this one is her backup—and she begged me to take her to Plain & Simple ("Modest Clothing for Modest Youth") to shop for a replacement. The veil is the official excuse for why we hauled all the way out to the Meadowlands Mallplex; the unofficial excuse is that I couldn't handle another minute trapped in the house with her as she went into raptures (not to be confused with *the* Rapture, which is one of her favorite topics) over the miracle of me. Of *us*.

I detoured at Babiez R U because I thought she would be a good audience for rehearsing the enthusiasm I need to pull off if I have any chance of taking over as president of the Pro/Am Pregg Alliance when my other best friend, Shoko Weiss, goes on birthleave.

The vice president and would-be successor, Malia Arroyo, is on what they call an indefinite leave of absence.

Speaking as her friend, I miss her.

But as her peer birthcoach, that's all I'm legally permitted to say on the subject.

Ventura Vida is running against me. She's new, so I've got seniority, but she's flaunting a twenty-four-week bump that is just too perfect and adorable not to vote for. Her family put her in private school when the public districts starting making all preggers drop out of regular high school to attend a special school where they're all brainwashed into keeping their deliveries. Gah. It's not quite as bad as Harmony having to get *married*, but can you imagine? Ventura aspires to be the first Southeast Asian–American woman elected president of the United States and views tomorrow's vote as the first of many on the path to the White House. All of this should make her an interesting person that I would otherwise want to get to know if it weren't for the unfortunate circumstance of her being a total powertrippy bitch.

Harmony is almost a welcome distraction from what I have to look forward to at school tomorrow. Just thinking about all the drama gets my tubes in a twist.

Harmony takes a deep breath, the veil sucking up her nose, then murmurs something to herself—a go-to inspirational verse, probably—before making a go at talking.

"Well!" Harmony repeats brightly. "How many weeks is . . . ?" She points in the general direction of my belly.

"Forty. And twins."

"Twins! Like us!"

"It makes a bold statement," I say, rotating in front of the mirrors. "A twin having twins."

Harmony sucks in another lungful of air. "So true, sister!"

I cringe from the inside out whenever she says that word. I can't change the fact that Harmony is my identical twin, but I don't know if I'll ever call this stranger my sister. Special emphasis on the strange part. I know Churchies are expected to fill their conversion quotas and all, but it was still a shock when Harmony asked if I had God within ten seconds of me answering the door.

"Do I have Him, like, in my *pocket*?" I had laughed, still stunned by her unannounced arrival.

"No, sister," she had said without a trace of irony. "In your *heart*."

I had gotten used to MiChatting with her a few times a week. Though she had extended countless invitations for me to visit her in Goodside—a trip I just wasn't ready to make—she had made no mention of crossing into Otherside to see me.

So this was just too much. I mean, how do you think

you'd feel if you opened the door at seven o'clock in the morning to see your exact double standing on your front porch, dressed all in white, clutching a shiny Bible in one hand and a banged-up suitcase in the other? I'm lucky I didn't terminate right then and there. For serious.

It wasn't until she hugged me ("Sister!") that I realized I wasn't hallucinating from a secondhand dose of Tocin. It really was Harmony on my doorstep. I wouldn't have been so neggy if Harmony had *asked* to visit me. I don't know the protocol for long-lost twin reunions or anything but at the very least she could have warned me.

All things considered, I think I've been handling things pretty well. I've come a long way since our first MiChat, when I barely managed to ask, "Harmony *who*? I'm your *what*?" I immediately quikiwikied the birth certificates that proved it wasn't a phishy scam and she really was my identical twin named Harmony who had set out to find her bioparents but found me instead. It's not like I *never* wanted to meet her in person, I'm just not up for making major media right now, and being a monozygotic twin always attracts attention even when they're not nearly as reproaesthetical as I am. (I mean, *we* are.)

I'm not being braggy. It's fact. I'm everything I'm supposed to be—attractive and intelligent, athletic and artistic, social and so on—only better. Ash and Ty, my parents, can't take credit for my natural-born assets but they do deserve recognition for all the time, money, energy, and effort they put into perfecting them. Even their surname—Mayflower—boosts my brand. And yet, these pluses can only go so far. What a relief it was when the results of my YDNA test confirmed that I am indeed *the* dying breed of a dying breed, rare and highly valued in certain Eurosnobby circles.

Harmony too.

That's another reason I was so put off this morning. It was one thing to hear her (my!) voice, but it was an entirely different thing to experience Harmony face-to-face. I eyeballed her blond hair and blue eyes, full lips and wide eyes, pert nose and high cheekbones, and panicked.

She's counterfeiting me!

Then I took in her white veil and neck-to-ankle gown and unclenched. The Church is extreme even by *ordinary* God-having standards, so Harmony is off market. I wanted to make sure.

"So you're set up," I said, "like, to be a wife and mother."

Harmony looked down at her gloved hands before answering. "Yes."

"That's great news," I answered, because it was—for me.

I could be living a totally different life right now. Harmony and I could—and probably should—have been raised together. We don't have many details, but from what we do know, it's pretty clear our biomom was damaged goods by the time she dropped us off. The musical names she picked out for us are proof enough of her pharmaceutically addled mind. We were born addicted to whatever junk she was on, and came out such sickly, shrieky preemies that the counselors from Good Shepherd Child Placement Services thought we had a better chance of being snapped up as singletons than as a janky twosome. Harmony was in worse shape than I was, and was taken in by the Church several weeks after I was placed with Ash and Ty.

My parents are beyond intense, but Harmony's off-grid upbringing has made me so thankful that mine adopted me and hers adopted her. With its ancient ivy-covered buildings, Princeton may not be the moddest hub on the Northeast Corridor but at least it just opened up an Underground All-Sports Arena and an Avatarcade. Harmony has spent her whole life in Goodside, Pennsylvania. She shares 6,500 square feet with three other families in one of the Starter Castles for Christ, those half-built McMansions in the never-finished gated enclaves bought dirt cheap by the Church in the late '00s. Harmony claims it's the largest settlement of its kind, which really isn't saying much when there's only a dozen or so in existence. The Church refers to the world beyond the Goodside gates as Otherside because it's subtle like that.

One thing I appreciate about Harmony is that I don't have to worry about encryption. Her immediate intentions are totally clear: She's here to make me get religion. And not just any religion, of course, but hers. If I'm married along with the rest of her housesisters by the end of the month, I think she scores some major bonus angel points toward a heavenly set of wings or a halo or something. Despite her invitations, I know I'm not welcome in Goodside and it's not because they fear HPSV. The Church is far more threatened by the possibility that I'll infect their minds with sin. I could flash my lab results proving that the damage has already been done to my reproductive system and there's no chance of catching the Virus from me, but they wouldn't even care. I was shocked when Harmony told me that they don't even *test* for the Virus in Goodside, because, as she explained, there is only one who can open and close the womb, and He flicks the switch from His heavenly throne. It's no mere coincidence then, as she also explained, that there are more women pregging in their twenties and thirties on her side of the gates than on mine.

Well. How can you argue against that?

harmony
melody

MELODY AND I CAME INTO THIS LIFE TOGETHER AND I'LL DO whatever it takes to see her in the next one. But, my grace, she's not making it easy.

I was surprised that she didn't even consider searching for her (our!) birthparents as soon as she came of age. That was my first order of business when I turned sixteen. She claims that she never sought the truth about our birthparents because it could bring more bad news than good.

"You weren't the least bit curious about who brought us into this world?"

"I've got the YDNA test results, and that's all I need to know," she replied. "Ash and Ty made me the person I am today."

I didn't understand this reaction at all. I've *always* felt the need to know the truth about my birthparents. I thought knowing them would help me better understand myself. Please don't think I'm disrespecting the Smith family by saying this. I don't remember when I was told that I was adopted, I can only say that I don't remember a time when I *didn't* know I was adopted. The Church has a long tradition of taking in the neediest infants—as it still does—and I was one of them. My parents were the angels entrusted with my care and protection and I'm forever grateful He chose them for me.

Always worried about my health, Ma never let me roughhouse and always lured me toward more meditative pursuits like baking and crafting. These skills, she knew, would serve me well when I turned thirteen and was picked for marriage in my Blooming. She taught me everything I know about what it means to be a good wife and mother, nourishing me with all the fruits of the spirit: joy, peace, kindness, faithfulness, and gentleness. What's happened to me since then isn't her fault. She did the best she could.

I wish more than anything I could tell her that right now.

Despite Ma's efforts, I've never felt . . . complete. I prayed and prayed and prayed. I asked why my birthparents had surrendered me and I got frustrated with Him for not answering. Until I knew, I would always feel like something—or someone—was missing no matter how hard or long or often I called on Him for help. Finally, after a difficult and dark period in my early Blooming, Ma took me aside and told me something I'll never forget.

"Prayers are answered in one of four ways," she said. *"Yes. No. I have something else in mind.* And . . ."

She paused long enough for my impatience to show. "And what's the fourth answer?"

"Wait," she said.

I realized that maybe I wasn't ready for the answers God had in store for me.

And so I patiently waited until my sixteenth birthday when it was legal for me to unseal my birth documents.

HARMONY DOE
Placement: SMITH
Born: 05-02-2020 (approximate)
Birth Father: UNKNOWN
Birth Mother: UNKNOWN
Relations: MELODY DOE [See: MAYFLOWER]
Notes: Infant twin females born at approximately 32
weeks; required NICU intervention for detoxification and
other development issues associated with preterm delivery;
anonymously given up to Princeton Medical Center pro-
fessionals in compliance with the New Jersey Safe Haven
Act with handwritten note reading: "Forgive me, Harmony
and Melody"; placed into permanent custody by the Good
Shepherd Family Placement Services.

I had a twin.

A twin.

The Heavens opened for me at that moment. A twin! What a revelation! I made a choice right then and there not to mourn for the unknown parents I had lost, but to celebrate the sister I had found. My whole life I thought I was praying for my birthparents. Suddenly I knew who I was really praying for: my twin. My sister. My other half. Though I didn't know my sister named Melody, I loved her already. Ma and Pa were never told about Melody and were even more stunned to find out about her than I was. Ma saw an opportunity to spread the Word.

"This is your purpose in life," Ma said. "Putting your sister on the right path for the next one."

I'm taking Ma's advice. Can I redeem myself if I bring Melody to Otherside to receive the sacraments? Despite her protests, I see the truth: Melody isn't sure of her decision to go pro. I know it. And if she spends more time in my company, perhaps she'll want to follow me in faith. And she, in turn, just might give me strength to be the wife and mother I've so far failed to be.

"Am I fertilicious?" she asks. "Or what?"

I love my sister unconditionally—even if she makes it difficult to like her. Watching her as she unabashedly admires herself in the mirror, I realize that I have a long, hard road ahead of me. If only my relationship with Melody was as effortless as my relationship with God. Talking to God isn't a chore. I can let my true self shine in front of God.

melody
harmony

"DO YOU KNOW WHO ELSE MAKES A BOLD STATEMENT?"
Harmony asks.

"God?" I try.

"Inspired answer, sis—!" Harmony stops herself short.
"Melody!"

It's Harmony's mission in life to put the "fun" back in
fundamentalism. She's never happier than when she's bragging on God. I'm about to tell her that she might want to
dose down a bit when the Babiez R U salesclerk ducks her
head through the pink-and-blue gingham curtains. Name
tag: TRYNN.

"You're glowing!" Trynn gushes.

I caress my stretchy belly with pride.

"God-mocking," chimes Harmony with cheery confidence.

Trynn is a skilled saleswoman and won't be put off by Churchy negs on her trade. She puts two hands on my tumescent tummy. "Can you feel the kicking?"

I can.

"And you'll note the tiny, tasteful stretch marks," she continues, lifting my brand-new expandable-contractable MyTurnTee.

Trynn looks to Harmony. "Are you interested in trying something on?"

Harmony primly pats her shoulder-length veil. "It's against my religion."

"Really? I wouldn't have guessed," Trynn says, stifling a snicker.

The clerk takes a step back to eye Harmony's ivory veil, which matches the crisp cotton cap-sleeved ball gown with a sweetheart neckline and brush-the-floor train. She'll wear a similar, if slightly fancier, gown on her wedding day, after which she'll wear green gowns symbolizing fertility, followed by pink or blue gowns—depending on the sex of her first child—to announce the fulfillment of her "feminine promise," as she put it.

Only engaged girls wear veils, which is supposed to deflect unwanted male attention. That might work in Goodside, but here it has the opposite effect. She gets more attention all covered up than I would if I went around flashing my breedy bits all day long.

"Oh, yes," says Harmony from behind the tulle scrim. "I'm just visiting. . . ." She tugs on the elbow-length glove covering her left hand.

"Is there a ring under there?"

Harmony stiffens for a moment then says, "Of course I'm wearing a ring!"

"Can we see it?" Trynn and I ask simultaneously.

"No," Harmony says curtly. It's a voice I haven't heard before. "Showing off is the sin of pride. . . ." Her voice trails off.

"What's his name?" I ask, realizing just now that in our MiChats Harmony gushed on and on about God, but didn't say one word about her fiancé.

"Ephraim," Harmony says

"Ephraim?" Trynn asks. "That's an unusual name."

"Not where I'm from. There are four Ephraims in our settlement. It means 'doubly fruitful.'"

"Like you!" Trynn points at my belly.

"Everyone calls him Ram."

"Ram, huh?" Trynn licks her lips. "That's a breedy name if I've ever heard one!"

I'm not sure if Trynn is mocking Harmony or not. The trubie gear makes her an easy target for anyone but especially for bitter obsolescents. Just when I'm starting to feel sorry for the salesclerk's squandered reproductivity, Trynn says something totally barren to Harmony.

"That engagement gown is so *pure*," she says gently.

"But aren't you, like, too *mature* to wear white? Shouldn't you be in the pink or blue by now?"

Harmony yelps from behind her veil. I can't see, but I imagine the blood draining from her face, until her pallid complexion matches her colorless dress. There's no way Trynn knew about the color-coded gowns without looking it up on the quikiwiki. She did it just to be neggy.

My face glows red with anger, which is weird because I barely know Harmony. I mean, we don't have anything in common, you know, besides our genetic material. I agreed to let her stay with me for a few days because Ash and Ty swear up and down that my heart-stopping story about long-lost twinbonding will help get me into Global U., a university so notoriously selective it makes Princeton look like a safety school. That's the only reason I didn't send her straight back to the farm this morning.

I know it's a scandal to say something like that, with multis like us being so prized and all. But the more Harmony talks, the more it becomes clear that the Church isn't giving much of a choice in the matter of marriage and motherhood. Zen says that she's trapped by her own false consciousness, which, by the way, is the nerdish kind of comment that could get a guy's ass kicked at our school—if that ass was anyone's but Zen's.

He's the only one who knows I've been in contact with Harmony. For as much as he loves to talk, he is surprisingly tight-lipped when he needs to be. As such, he's the keeper of many of Princeton Day Academy's deepest secrets. Of course, that doesn't stop him from privately warning me that coming into identical twinhood at sixteen will for seriously damage my fragile psyche or whatever. But it hasn't. *Harmony's* the one who stalked our bioparents. She's the one having the identity crisis, not me. These days the majority of deliveries in this country aren't raised by their bioparents, and they should all follow my example by having the same attitude.

Don't fit me for a veil or anything because I can be sympathetic to Harmony and still have issues with her way of life. But before I have a chance to put the salesclerk in her place, Harmony breaks the awkward silence.

"I was engaged at thirteen years old."

What?! She never said a word about her starter engagement! At thirteen I wasn't even close to making my own commitment, no matter how much parental pressure I was under. Which was a *lot*.

"But God had another plan!" Harmony adds a bit too eagerly. "I keep telling my sis—" She stops herself. "I keep telling *Melody* that it's not too late for her to get a husband. There are plenty of eligible bachelors in Goodside."

I snort-laugh. Harmony is just too funny. Sometimes I wonder if Church leaders are slipping Tocin or some other prescription-strength love drug into the sacramental wine.

Trynn turns to me. "I assume *you're* here for nostalgia's sake," she says, still hoping to make the sale. "Let me guess. You're in between bumps and want to relive the best nine months of your life?"

I reluctantly flash back to Malia.

"The worst nine months of my life!" she howled. *"For what?"*

I hate thinking of her in that state.

I open my mouth but nothing comes out.

Harmony mutters another prayer and hooks an arm around my shoulder. And as much as I know that she's doing this just to prove that she's the kindhearted twin, I'm comforted by the gesture.

"My extra thirty is oh so flirty!" chirp voices outside the dressing room.

A tweenage trio comes swaggering into the dressing room. The tweens accessorize their sparkly Ts with matching First Curse Purses, the menarche must-have for stashing the pads and tampons they'll need *any minute now.* The target demo for Babiez R U, they steal Trynn's attention.

"I see you're considering the Preggerz FunBump with real skinfeel and in-uterobic activity!" she says to the one with red hair holding up the fake belly she's ready to try on. The front of the redhead's T reads: DO THE DEED. As she hops around in excited circles, I catch the phrase on the back: BORN TO BREED.

Indeed.

"She's wearing size Forty-Week Twins," Trynn continues, pointing to my distended stomach. "That's way too big for you! Size Twenty-four-Week Singleton is perfect for a girl your age. . . ."

I think of Ventura Vida's adorable six-month bump and a wave of nausea rolls right over me. Harmony can't pass up another opportunity to get preachy.

"When I was your age," she offers, "I was leading my own prayerclique!"

The twelve-year-olds giggle nastily.

That's it. I terminate. I skulk behind the curtains, strip off the Preggerz FunBump, and hang it on the wall hook. I had come here today hoping that the experience would help me feel breedier than I did before Malia's meltdown, but all I've done is remind myself just how far behind I am. Unburdening myself of the fake belly does little to improve my state of mind. The MyTurnTee shrinks to fit my taut abdominals and my mood shrivels with it.

Harmony peeks behind the curtain. "Can we please head over to Plain & Simple now?"

"Sure thing." And before I can stop myself: "Maybe there's a sale on tasteful straitjackets."

It was a for seriously pissy thing to say. I don't know why I'm taking out my frustration on her.

Harmony clasps her hands and quietly sighs behind the veil. "Oh my grace."

She lifts her veil so I can see her face. It takes my breath away whenever she does this. It's surprisingly easy to forget that there's another person on the planet who was born looking *exactly* like me, only frecklier. Harmony gestures for me to lean in closely to hear what she has to say.

"Pursue faith and love and peace," she says in a quiet

but confident voice. "Enjoy the companionship of those who call on the Lord with pure hearts."

Harmony lets the veil fall back over her face, pulls the curtains together, and leaves me alone to consider her biblical wisdom.

The FunBump squirms against the back of the dressing-room wall, and one of the twins' elbows or maybe a knee pokes out of the bogus belly. What felt like an organic extension of my own body just moments ago now makes me more squeamish than my worst case of Sympathetic Morning Sickness. I stab my finger deep into the belly on/off button more aggressively than necessary and the FunBump goes limp.

"You're knocked up," sing the little girls along with the incessant Babiez R U theme song. *"Ready to pop, due to drop."*

It's hard not to get jealous of these nubie-pubies who—if they're pretty enough, smart enough, and healthy enough—should already be getting wooed by RePro Representatives. Those were the *best* times, when I was still all promise and potential. Because right now I'm definitely *not* the most important sixteen-year-old on the planet. Not even ish. I'm just another prebumped girl dangerously close to wasting her prime reproductivity.

Since the nubie-pubies caught me by surprise, I check my MiNet. I'm not expecting to spot anyone I know when—gah!—I get a positive MiD.

harmony
melody

I'M BEING PATIENT, KEEPING AN OPEN HEART, FORGIVING Melody for her participation in the buying and selling of blasphemous synthetic blessings when she comes running out of the dressing room blind-wild as a beheaded chicken.

"I can be anywhere but here!" she cries in a mad dash for the door.

Praise the Lord. Could it be I'm already having a positive influence on her?

"Wait for me!" I'm struggling to keep up with her, briefly regretting my decision to wear this particular gown. It's difficult to walk, let alone run. Such are the challenges when one is expected to serve as a powerful example of faith and female purity.

"Melody!"

I'm starting to think that I will never catch up when I hear a tenor voice behind me calling the same name.

"Melody!"

A whiplike figure streaks past me, quickly overtakes my sister, and stops right in her path. She screeches to a halt in front of an archway of red, white, and blue balloons. It's clear even at a distance that this boy with big hair and even bigger grin has done what I couldn't: made her burn with embarrassment.

I catch up to them at the patriotic display at the entrance to the U.S. Buff-A.

"The Meadowlands Mallplex has five million square feet of commercial enterprise and destination entertainment," the boy says, waving his arms at the stores all around us. "What are the odds of me *randomly* stumbling into your facespace?"

"None." She's pressing her lips together to stop herself from catching the boy's contagious grin. I'm smiling at him and I don't even *know* him. "I haven't seen you for, like, *ever*, and now all of a sudden you get stalky on me? How did you even find me here anyway? I blinded my MiNet."

The boy's smile gets bigger. And so does mine.

"Your MiNet blind is an insult to hackers everywhere."

"You hacked my MiNet?" She sounds more amazed than annoyed. "Again?"

The boy and Melody are exactly the same height, though the tips of his hair—dark and spiky like sprigs of

29

blackrot rosemary—give him an extra few inches. He only has to take a step toward her to look her straight in the eyes.

"Blink-left-right-left-wink-double-blink," as his eyes follow those same commands. Melody gasps, squeezes her eyes tight, and sighs in resignation. He, having made the desired impact, takes a step back and thumbs in my direction. "Is that *her*?"

"No," Melody says drily. "That's the third sister, Symphony. And there are two more at home who look just like her named Rhythm and Tempo."

"When did she get here?" he asks. "Why didn't you tell me she was coming?"

"I didn't tell you because I didn't know she was on her way. And also because you've been too busy to reply to any of my messages."

"Oh."

"Yeah."

"Sorry."

The boy looks at me, then back at Melody.

"You must be blinked."

"You think?"

I am waiting patiently to share my own feelings about seeing my twin for the first time, but no one is asking.

"How long will she be in town?" He asks this as if I've got limited seating, like when Brother Moses' Traveling Ministry finally came to Goodside.

"We're still . . . um . . ." She coughs and casts me a sidelong glance. "Working out the details."

I've told Melody I'm willing to stay with her until she's ready to return to Goodside with me. She was so over-whelmed by emotion that she choked on her reply.

"Welcome to Otherside!" The boy sweeps his arms through the air. "I'm Zen Chen-Chavez." He extends his hand.

I tug on my gloves, fixing my fingers inside the satin.

"I'm . . . Harmony."

"You hesitated," Zen says, wiggling the fingers on his still-extended hand. "Is it against the rules to touch me?"

Zen is certainly observant. I admit that I am a bit leery of making physical contact with a free male because such touching *is* against Church Orders. But I'm not in Good-side, am I? And it's not like I'm touching skin to skin!

I answer Zen by taking his hand in mine and giving it a firm shake.

"Tell me," he says, giving me his full attention now. "How do you feel about all the premarital sex and sin?"

I'm supposed to think he's showing off for my benefit, but I can tell that it's really for Melody. And yet I can't find a way of answering his question.

"I don't know," I finally say.

"You could have learned a lot from watching the Cheerclones and the Ballers in action last night," he says.

"Ugh. MasSEXtinction parties are nasty," Melody says, scrunching her nose. "Those amateurs are so desperate."

Zen clucks his tongue. "How can you be the next Pro/Am president if you neg any girl who doesn't have

31

a contract? You have to promote positive pregging in *all* forms."

"Yeah, yeah, I know," Melody says dismissively. "I still can't believe you went last night."

"*Someone* had to be the designated driver," he says. "I was the only one who didn't get dosed."

"So," Melody says, avoiding Zen's gaze. "Does that mean you were the only one on the sidelines during the group grope?"

If Zen notices the strain in her voice, he doesn't let on.

"You of all people know I hold myself up to the highest standards," he says. "Unfortunately, this means I'll never bump with any girl who is desperate enough to bump with me."

This makes my sister laugh-snort-laugh, which makes me laugh-snort-laugh because—PTL!—we share the same laughy-snorty laugh!

Both Zen and Mel turn to me with surprised expressions, as if they'd forgotten I was standing right beside them.

"How do you feel about wearing that gown?" Zen asks. "Can you take off your veil?"

I remember being faced with such unenlightenment in my previous trips to Otherside with my prayerclique. For a group who clings so desperately to facts, seculars like Zen and Mel understand so very little about the Church. I cherish this chance to witness because there are so few opportunities to do so in a settlement where everybody—well, *almost* everybody—is already saved. It's vital for me to approach this in the right way so I don't scare him off.

"Oh my grace, those are inspired questions," I reply, mindful of my tone. "Before I answer, may I ask you a question first?"

"Sure," Zen says. "I love questions."

"Do you have God?"

He answers with uncommon directness. "I don't."

I had anticipated that response, but all witnessing must begin with the basics.

"Now that I've answered your question," Zen says, "I hope you'll answer mine."

"Well," I say, smoothing over the wrinkles in my dress, "I'm proud to serve as a powerful example of faith and female purity." I wince, worried about sounding vain. "And, yes, I'm allowed to take off my veil whenever I want."

"Why don't you take it off right now?" Zen asks.

"Because I don't want to."

I really don't. I have full control over my words but my positive messaging is often undone by negative facial expressions. This has become more clear to me since joining Melody's company. I see her pursed lips, flared nostrils, or arched eyebrows on our shared face, revealing her true feelings as they would certainly reveal mine. Meeting Melody has convinced me that wearing the veil was the right thing.

"I don't blame you for not taking it off. Some people say

the lower rates of HPSV in your community are because you get extra protection from the veils and gloves," he says, looking down at his hands. "Maybe we'd all be fertile into our twenties and thirties if we wore them."

"Or maybe it's all the *prayer* that keeps the Virus at bay," Melody offers sarcastically.

That's exactly what the Church Council claims.

"It's just a shame you won't take it off," Zen says to me with a shrug. "It would have been such a pleasure to be seen with *two* reproaesthetical girls."

"Careful, Zen, you're talking to a soon-to-be-married woman here." Melody is trying to sound lighthearted, but, as always, her face gives her away.

"I guess I'll just have to settle for half the pleasure," Zen says, ignoring her warning.

"For serious, Zen. Harmony's fiancé is named Ram."

Zen stares in disbelief. "Ram?"

"Ram. And he's a genuine agriculty." Melody's voice is turning now too. "He could ride up on his horse and kick your sorry butt all the way down the turnpike."

I let out a little yelp at the visual of Ram kicking *anyone's* you-know-what.

"Is that true?" Zen asks. "That Ram will kick my sorry butt to defend your honor?"

"No," I say simply, biting my lip to stop myself from giggling.

Ram is almost a foot taller than Zen and quite fit from farming, but he would never act in such a way. If

Ram were here right now, it would be customary for him to thank Zen for his approving appraisal of my physical appearance, then gently point out that it is inappropriate for any man to pay such compliments to another man's woman. But it's unlikely Ram would say this or much of anything else because it's against his nature to be confrontational. "Blessed are the peacemakers," says Ma about Ram. "For they shall be called sons of God."

"This has been fun," Zen says, his face suddenly straight and serious. "But I actually do have a reason for stalking you today. And it's kind of ironic too, considering what we were just talking about. . . ."

Melody squints. "Okay." She sounds skeptical.

Zen takes a piece of paper out of his back pocket, unfolds it, and holds it up for her inspection.

"Does *this* mean anything to you?"

Melody startles at the sight of it.

It clearly holds some significance for her.

And whatever it is, it's not good.

melody
harmony

FOUR YEARS AGO TODAY, MANDATORY BLOOD TESTS confirmed that 75 percent of sixth through eighth graders at Princeton Day Academy Junior School had been infected with the Virus. Most parents hoped it was the unfunniest prank ever. Mine anticipated the spread of the Virus all along and had planned accordingly. Even though I'd heard Ash and Ty talk about Human Progressive Sterility Virus millions of times before, I never really understood what the words meant.

Zen knew. He had done his research. Even then he liked to be informed, even if such knowledge was the stuff of nightmares.

He made me watch a video that explained what had happened to us, or, more accurately, what *wouldn't* happen: that we were among the roughly three-quarters of the planet who wouldn't be able to conceive or carry a full-term delivery in adulthood. Most of us would go irreversibly infertile sometime between our eighteenth and twentieth birthdays, and petri-pregging wouldn't be a viable option for us at any age. The video was called *The End of the World as We Know It* and it succeeded in making me so paranoid about what would happen to our depopulated nation—with a special emphasis on the inevitable takeover by the awesomely abundant Chinese—that I signed this letter of promise:

> *Zen Chen-Chavez and Melody Mayflower promise that if both of us have NOT made a delivery within the next four years, we will bump with each other. This agreement is voided if one of us (Zen!!!) says ANYTHING about it to ANYONE!!!*

To understand why I would sign such a document, you have to understand Zen.

See, Zen has always prided himself on being able to analyze and argue all sides of any issue. It's what makes him one of the top high school debaters in the state. I'm his best friend, so I know he doesn't believe half of what comes out of his mouth or across his MiNet profile. But he's so effortlessly persuasive that even I'm not always sure what half he believes and what half is bullshit. He knows what to say, when to say it, how to say it, and to whom.

These skills have served him well at Princeton Day Academy: Everyone loves him.

I think we became best friends because I was one of the very few kids who didn't do what he said.

"Why aren't you calling yourself Lem?" he asked on the day he made everyone refer to themselves by the backward spellings of their first names.

"Why should I call myself Lem just because you want me to," I replied. *"Nez."*

Zen loved that. He thought I was cool because I had a mind of my own. Only later, much later, did he discover the exact opposite was true and I wasn't a nonconformist by choice. No, Ash and Ty already had me on such an uncompromising regimen of self-improvement that there was simply no time in my life for Zen's ridiculous diversions.

Of course, my pact with Zen wasn't ridiculous. It was dead serious. And in my limited worldview at the time, it was the first time Zen's directives were totally worth following.

And yet, the letter was already a distant memory when I signed on with Lib at UGenXX Talent Agency a year later. Right away, I started getting major swag from the most affluential couples desperate for me to make a healthy delivery. At thirteen, I was boosting off the free merch and the surge in eyeballs on my MiNet profile but was in no way ready to settle down. By the time I was fourteen, my parents thought I was obsessed with famegaming and at risk of becoming terminally starcissistic if I didn't close a deal soon. Later that year I was matched with the Jaydens, who put in a very strong bid: full college tuition, a Volkswagen Plug, *and* a postpartum tummy trim. When Lib pushed—and got—a six-figure signing bonus, there was no question as to what I had to do.

It's hard to believe now, but this was a pretty radical decision at the time. Though popular in major cities on the coasts, going pro was still kind of a down-market thing to do in the suburbs, and at my school in particular. All preggers at Princeton Day Academy were amateurs, most of whom put deliveries up for nonprofit adoptions. I can count on one hand how many actually kept their deliveries, and those who did had them raised by the same nannies who had raised them.

Ash and Ty are—or *were*—Wall Streeters turned economics professors at the University who were way ahead of reproductive trends. They predicted sixteen years ago, almost before anyone else, that girls like me—prettier, smarter, healthier—would be the world's most valuable resource. And like any rare commodity in an unregulated marketplace, prices for our services would skyrocket. It wasn't about the money, really, not at first. It was about status. Who had it, and who didn't. And my parents did everything in their power to make sure I had it.

As for me, I figured, *Why not? I won't be using my uterus for anything else during those nine months!* So that's how I was the first girl in my class to go pro and sign on to be a Surrogette. About a dozen girls at my school have followed my lead so far, with more trying to land contracts every day. Now even amateurs who aren't quite upmarket enough to go pro can make decent money at auction if their deliveries earn high marks from Newborn Quality Testing Service.

The point is, Ash and Ty knew that if anyone could boost the image of commerical pregging in our community, it was me. It's what they groomed me for, after all.

And my life has been ectopic ever since.

Only Zen would try to legitimize a pact between two twelve-year-old nubie-pubies who pretended to be more familiar with the how-tos of pregging than we actually were.

Only Zen would have any chance at succeeding.

harmony
melody

"WHAT IS IT?" I ASK.

"Nothing," Melody quickly replies, pinching the paper distastefully with her thumb and forefinger as she hands it back to Zen. He carefully smooths out the paper, refolds it along the original creases, and slides it into his back pocket before responding.

"I never pegged you for a renegger . . ."

The calmer Zen is, the more emotional my sister gets.

"I am NOT a renegger. You are beyond wanked if you think that piece of paper is binding. . . ."

I'm not following this at all.

Then, like the sun bursting through storm clouds, that grin.

"Dose down, Mel. I'm just scamming." Zen's cheeks

dimple even deeper. "I really came by just to say 'hey.'"

Melody eyes him warily. "So say it."

"Say what?"

Now it's Melody's turn to take a step forward, lean in, and get within a few inches of his face.

"Hey."

At first, Zen doesn't move. Then slowly, almost imperceptibly, he brings his face even closer to my sister's. I watch his lips part and I watch Melody's expression change to something expectant and—

Oh my grace! Stop watching!

I turn my head left. Newlywed Bliss Kits are on sale at Garden of Eden Sex Shop. . . .

Look away!

I turn my head right. The young trio from Babiez R U is immodestly strutting by us, flaunting their brand-new FunBumps. . . .

Close . . . your . . . eyes!

But I can't. I can't. I can't. *I can't stop watching.* I can't stop watching Melody and Zen as they hypnotically hover almost—*almost!*—mouth to mouth. . . .

"Hey," Zen whispers.

I'm startled by a sharp, high cry. Both by the sound and the fact that it came from me.

Melody and Zen lurch away from each other.

"YOU BLINKED FIRST!" they cry in unison.

Zen turns to me as if he wants me to vouch for him, but then his face darkens.

"Whoa. Are you feeling okay? You're breathing heavy. And your skin—what I can see of it—is all red and sweaty."

He's right. I'm feeling a little light-headed. "I'm f-f-f-fine," I stammer, fanning myself. "It gets hot under all these layers."

Melody is patting her hair, trying to look unconcerned. "Oh, it's nothing that a cold can of Coke '99 can't fix."

Zen seems genuinely worried. "You should really take off that veil. . . ."

"Enough about the mutherhumping veil," Melody says in a cold voice. *"She's not going to take it off."*

I don't want to take off my veil, but I can't catch my breath. I lift the netting from my face and flip it up and over my head so I can get some air. I shield my eyes until they adjust to the riot of light and color. I forget how much brighter the world looks without the veil. I avert my gaze from the Garden of Eden Sex Shop.

"Sweet Darwin's revenge," Zen says, eyes going wide at the sight of my bare face. "You're Melody!"

Oh my grace. If there's one thing I've already learned about my twin, it's that she does not like being seen as anything less than unique. I square my shoulders, ready for Melody to explode at Zen. Ma taught me to only raise my voice in praise, never in anger. Despite her musical name, my sister gives little thought to the sounds that come out of her mouth. She doesn't seem to understand that words can serve as a bomb *or* a balm and all too often Melody chooses to hurt instead of heal. This time she surprises me.

Her words come out not in a ferocious rush, but slowly, like ice.

"She . . . is . . . not . . . me."

I proceed very carefully. "She's right!" I say. "I have freckles!"

"You do?" Zen squints at my nose. "You do!"

Zen can't stop looking back and forth between us, comparing and contrasting and comparing and contrasting our faces. And he's not the only one. A small crowd has gathered around us, all winking, blinking, and rolling their eyeballs in our direction. I know that as I stand here contemplating my freckles, images of the identical-but-ideodemographically different twins are already streaming the MiNet. This must be what Melody means when she refers to a surge in optics—but I don't feel too good about it. It makes me squirmy, like a soilworm under observation in a terrarium. I pull my veil back over my face to put an end to it.

"I imagine this must be quite a change from your settlement," Zen says.

"Yes it is," I say. Then to provide an example of tolerance, I add, "I watched Melody try on FunBumps at Babiez R U."

Zen's enthusiasm wanes for the first time during this conversation. My sister takes in Zen's stricken face, and seems to find courage in it. She continues with a new gleam in her eye.

"I was, um . . ." She casts a quick glance in the direction

of Babiez R U for inspiration. "*Fertilicious*, wasn't I?"

Again, the word sounds false coming out of her mouth. And yet it still causes Zen to tug on his hairspikes. His obvious distress emboldens my sister even more.

"Wasn't I?"

I don't agree with what my sister is saying, but I want her to like me. She gives up when I take too long to corroborate.

"Oh well," she says with a shrug, "I'm done here. I'm taking the shuttle home."

No! This is going all wrong.

"But what about my veil?" I ask, trying to stay calm.

"If you need it so badly, why don't you go back to Goodside and get it?" She hesitates for a moment as if she knows she shouldn't say what she's about to say, but decides to say it anyway. "Maybe you should go back to Goodside, where you belong."

Where I belong. If she only knew.

"But . . ." I say, trying not to well up. "I hoped . . ."

"What? That I would give up everything I've got here and go back with you? That I would settle down and get married and make"—she spits out the last word—"*babies*?"

She's right. I had hoped—unrealistically so, I now see—that my blood sister would share Ma's and my housesisters' enthusiasm for marriage and motherhood. But Melody is nothing like the girls in Goodside. No, her reluctance to fulfill her feminine promise makes her so much more like . . .

45

Me.

I gasp at the similarity. "Sister!"

Melody looks like she's just been kicked in the chest. Oh my grace, I've said it again! She quickly rights herself, and without so much as even a careless farewell to me or Zen, spins around and speeds toward the nearest exit.

"Later!" Zen calls out, admirably unaffected.

I'm not ready to leave yet. There's too much more I need to learn about my sister, and Zen is the person who can teach me. I'm nervous, but the spirit moves me to put my mission before myself.

"Zen," I say before my tongue gets stuck. "Would you care to escort me to Plain & Simple?"

I've never been so bold with a boy—not even Ram. Church girls do *not* initiate. I know it's an innocent invitation, and yet my face burns hotter than you-know-what.

Zen rakes his fingers through his hair. "Are you sure your fiancé won't get jealous?"

"My fiancé? Oh, no. No! He won't mind at all!"

This is true. Ram would never get jealous because such expressions of envy go against our faith.

"'Let us behave decently as in the daytime,'" I say out loud. When I notice Zen is clenching his jaw, I keep the rest of the verse to myself.

"'*Not in sexual immorality*,'" I mouth silently, leading Zen down the causeway. "'*Not in debauchery*.'"

melody

harmony

"SO AFTER DELETING HIMSELF FROM MY LIFE FOR WEEKS, HE totally stalks me at the Mallplex just to let me know that he chauffeured a bunch of Cheerclones to one of their nasty masSEX parties. He's crazy if he thinks he can make me, like, *jealous* or something. . . ."

I'm home now, venting to my friend Shoko on the MiVu. She's totally couched, crunching her way through a bag of Folato Chips . . . *now with 250 percent more folic acid*!

"And then he busts out this bogus contract from when we were, like, *twelve* that says that if we haven't bumped anybody by now we're obligated to bump each other. . . ."

"Mmmm . . ." Shoko murmurs with her mouth full. Due to drop any day now, she looks like a Eurasian grass snake that swallowed the moon. When she shifts slightly in the pillows—no small task at her size—an invisible woman's voice bursts into the room.

"*AZUL* . . . BLUE . . . *ROJA* . . . RED . . ."

"Oy!" Shoko lifts up her shirt to reveal the HeadStart belly band straining against her midsection. "Where's the volume on this damn thing?!"

"*AMARILLO* . . . YELLOW . . ."

She scrambles to find the smartpod that slipped between her butt and the couch cushions and jabs at the volume until the invisible Spanish teacher fades away.

"*VERDE* . . . GREEN . . . *MORADO* . . . PUR-PLE . . ."

"Oy, I can't wait until Burrito and I part ways."

Burrito is the nickname for her pregg. This is Shoko's first go as a pro. She bumped as an amateur last time around, which meant *she* picked her partner—her boy-friend, Raimundo—a RePro Rep didn't do it for her. It also meant that she didn't get paid up front like I did, but had to wait and see what offers came in after her deliv-ery was made. Unlike the Cheerclones and other amateurs who hit the masSEX party circuit hoping to be bumped, Shoko's first pregging wasn't *planned*, but it wasn't unex-pected either because that's what happens when boyfriends and girlfriends do what they do as often as Shoko and Raimundo did.

Both bright, brown-eyed brunettes with pleasing if asymmetrical facial features, Shoko and Raimundo are above average across the board, but nothing that would inspire Lib or any other RePro Rep to make six-figure promises. Shoko had never been seriously wooed to go pro, so it was a bit of a surprise when there was unusually competitive postdelivery auction. The winning bidders were so thrilled with the outcome that they hired Shoko to bump with Raimundo again (they were broken up at this point, which made it waaaay awkward but business is business and pleasure is pleasure), so the second pregg she's carrying now is biosiblings with the first. She's signed an option agreement to try for a third pregg, though with her eighteenth birthday just a month away, it's not a sure thing. Even without number three, she's earning enough money to cover her first year at Rutgers, which makes her way better off than she was before she got the first plus sign on her pee stick.

She's ready to pop, so I need to get into maternity mode. I was honored when she asked me to be her peer birthcoach because she's two years older and the Pro/Am president. She could have asked *anyone* in the Alliance for support. Choosing me—the only prebump among us— was a bold statement. And sticking with me after what happened to Malia . . . Well, that was even bolder.

But that's Shoko. She's not afraid to say what she thinks, and she never worries whether what she says will affect her image. We met when I was the youngest player to make the Little Tigers elite travel soccer team, the only girl in sixth grade good enough to compete with eighth grad- ers. The older girls got pissy when I not only kept up, but kicked circles around them. They wanted to haze me hard and threatened to cut off my ponytail to serve as a warning to other upstart sixth graders, but Shoko wouldn't let them. She's the one who stood up for me.

"If she's kicking *our* asses," she pointed out, "imagine what she'll do to the other team."

Since that moment on the soccer field, I've looked up to her like the big sister I never had.

Not that I've told her about the sister I *do* have. Shoko doesn't need my DNA drama to distract her from her contractual obligations. Not that that's stopped me from ranting about Zen.

"Okay. So where was I?" I ask myself. "Oh, right. Zen . . ."

Shoko sighs and sets down her bag of chips.

"I don't get it," she says.

"Get what?"

"Why Zen isn't your everythingbut." She runs her tongue over her teeth. "I hear Zen gives *gooooood* everythingbut."

I feel my face burn. "Heard it from *who*?"

"Ooooh," Shoko says. "Burrito's squatting on my sciatic nerve, but that's nothing like the nerve I just struck in *you*."

"Seriously." I grit my teeth into a smile. "Who? One of the Cheerclones?"

The Cheerclones are the varsity cheerleaders who are impossible to tell apart by design. For high-scoring uniformity in competitions, they're all within one-half inch in height (five three) and two and half pounds in weight (105 pounds). They've all dyed their hair and skin to match the average hair color and skin tone for the squad as a whole. For serious, they are virtually identical from their ponytails to their pedicures—it would be easier to tell me apart from my twin. Unlike Harmony and me, however, they're as predictably identical in thought as they are in appearance. They think, speak, and handspring as a unit, so it's no surprise they tried to pregg as one last night.

I still can't believe Zen went out with them. Gah.

"Why does it matter who?" Shoko says. "Ash and Ty have made you totally paranoid about the perfect bump! You're afraid that if you let a guy so much as *kiss* you, you'll break your hymen, break your contract, and ruin everything you've worked for your whole life."

She's right. I hate that she's right. But she is.

"What's taking the Jaydens so long anyway?" Shoko says, licking green Folato Chip dust off her thumb. "I thought Lib said you'd be bumped by the end of your sophomore year for sure."

Lib assures me that I'm everything they want in an Egg. I look almost exactly like the Mrs. did at my age only I'm a little bit taller, which ups my value, of course. And they're so impressed with my IQ and EQ scores. The problem has always been with the Sperm. They haven't found a donor that is a perfect match for the Mr., only with less hair in his ears and more on his head.

"Lib says the Mrs. is trying to persuade her husband to go totally commercial," I say. "She wants to invest big money in a top man brand. . . ."

Shoko clutches the empty bag to her chest. "Like Fitch or Phoenix from the Tocin ads?"

These RePros have all become famous for popping up on the MiNet more naked than not, seductively cooing: *"Can't bump with me? Fake it with a dose of Tocin."* Tocin makes you feel like your best and most reproaesthetical self, and see everyone around you in the same artificially flattering way. Originally touted as "the Peacemaker" for its potential to end conflict in the Middle East, it's now the most popular medication prescribed by doctors for Surrogettes and Sperms. Taken as directed, it helps "exaggerate feelings of arousal and attachment" and "ease the awkwardness and anxiety" of bumping with a total stranger.

Don't get me wrong. The Tocin models are seriously reproaesthetical, but their famegaming turns me off.

"I don't know," I say cautiously. "Maybe."

"Or Jondoe!" Shoko falls back in the pillows in full swoon. "I'd pregg decatuplets with him!"

"Shoko!" She really is too much.

"Hey, if you're gonna get paid to pregg, it might as well be with the best man brand in the business!"

Shoko's getting far more excited by this prospect than I am. I mean, it's difficult to imagine what doing it will be like when I don't know who I'll be doing it with. After all this buildup, I can only assume that the Jaydens will finally pick someone who is—at the very least—as reproaesthetical as I am. In that case, doing it will be totally worth the wait.

At least I hope so.

"Well, they haven't made up their minds," I say, "And until they do . . ."

"Let Zen be your everythingbut!"

"Good*bye*, Shoko . . ."

"EVERYTHINGBUT!"

I shut her down before she can say another word.

I can't help but notice a new message from Malia. It's the seventh in as many days. This time I delete it without even watching. And though I know it's irresponsible—Shoko's water could break at any moment—I blind my MiNet for the rest of the night.

Honestly? I think Shoko might be better off in the delivery room without me.

I mean, in an emergency situation, what more can I do for her that I couldn't do for Malia?

harmony
melody

ZEN AND I ARE SEATED IN A BOOTH AT THE U.S. BUFF-A. A waitress has just delivered the cheesesteak I ordered in honor of my home state. I adjust the netting on my veil so I can eat. She stands to the side and stares.

"Why don't you just take it off?"

It's an honest question, really. One with a complicated answer.

"Because she doesn't want to," Zen says brightly before turning back to me. "Besides, white really works for you." His gaze lingers on me long enough to require a trip to the confessional.

I blush. I'm not used to such flatteries. I know it's unreasonable for me to expect Ram to behave like Zen or any other Othersider. It would be sacrilegious if he did. I'm about to thank Zen for the compliment when he blinks and squeezes his eyes as if a cloud of busy gnats has just flown right into them. As quick as it starts, it stops.

"So why get married now?" he asks. "I mean, from everything I've read on the quikiwiki, it seems that girls in the Church are usually married around thirteen. . . ."

Unlike the salesgirl, who was using this information to mock me, Zen seems genuinely curious. I decide to take a leap of faith.

"I was engaged for the first time at thirteen."

Zen nods, not a trace of condescension or scorn on his face.

"And what happened to the first fiancé?"

What happened was 1 Corinthians.

The wife's body does not belong to her alone but also to her husband. In the same way, the husband's body does not belong to him alone but also to his wife. Do not deprive each other.

When I was thirteen and newly betrothed, my house-sisters and I studied this verse in prayerclique. It was the last sentence that I didn't get, as "deprive" implied that doing without marital relations would be like doing without food or water or another life-sustaining necessity. I couldn't imagine feeling this way about Shep, my first fiancé. He was three years older and I secretly called him "Sheep" because of his woolly beard, bleating laugh, and fondness for chewing on long blades of grass. I didn't know much else about him than that, really. We'd certainly never kissed, never even held hands. And yet it would only be a matter of weeks before my body belonged to him and his belonged to me.

Inspired by 1 Corinthians, I asked my housesisters a question that I had wanted to ask for a very long time.

"Are any of you afraid of . . . *consummating* the marriage?"

My housesisters' cheeks caught ablaze like a wildfire in a windstorm.

"But children are God's best gift!" said Mary.

"The fruit of the womb is His greatest legacy!" said Lucy.

"I'm not talking about childbirth," I cut in. "I'm talking about the *marital act*, the *bodily sharing* that leads to childbirth. . . ."

They avoided my eyes and murmured prayers I couldn't make out.

"None of you are afraid of what it will *feel* like to become one flesh? The *pain*?"

And Annie, the only girl our age still waiting for a betrothal, the housesister so scared of being left behind, the one who had been conspicuously quiet throughout this conversation, finally spoke.

"In Genesis, God says, *'With pain you will give birth to children. Your desire will be for your husband, and he will rule over you.'"*

Mary and Lucy murmured amens to that.

I wanted to explain to Zen how my housesisters' reactions underscored the secret fears I'd been having since I began my Blooming. The Church promises that there's no greater way for young women to please God than to take the sacraments. But the closer I got to my own marriage and maternity, the more I felt like I was only as praiseworthy as my healthy womb.

Why was I the only one who seemed to see it this way?

Orders require us to put the Church before ourselves. It was this sacrificial argument that Ma repeated whenever I had expressed my doubts about marrying someone I didn't love. Both times.

"What does JOY stand for?" she'd ask. "Jesus first. Others next. Yourself last . . ."

"What happened?" Zen asks again.

I look at him through the haze of tulle. "He married someone else."

Less than two weeks after that conversation with my housesisters, Annie exchanged vows with Shep alongside Mary and Lucy. It was Annie who would share a marital bed in their household, Annie who would give Shep a son with golden red hair, Annie who would be pregnant now with his second child. Annie, and not me.

"Why?"

"The Church Council decided I wasn't ready."

It was another three years before the Church gave me my second—and last—chance to set things right. With Ram. Another boy I could only love in a brotherly way.

"And are you ready now?" Zen's got a penetrating

gaze, as if he's trying to see through the veil and straight into my eyes.

"I have to be," I say. "I *will* be."

And then I take a huge, messy bite of my sandwich to discourage Zen from asking any more questions. We chew in silence for a few moments before I muster the courage to ask him a question of my own.

"Do all Surrogettes and Sperms get along like you and Melody do?"

"*What?*"

Those are the terms Melody used in our MiChats. Right away I get the impression that I've used them incorrectly, and that I've just asked a question as unenlightened as those Zen had asked me earlier. I press on nonetheless.

"You have a conception contract, right?"

"You think *I've* been *hired* to bump with *Melody*?"

I nod.

"You think I'm a *professional*?"

I nod again with fire-branded cheeks.

"Oh, Harmony." Zen laughs ruefully. "I'm not upmarket enough to be a RePro."

"A RePro?" I ask.

"Reproductive professional," he says, looking down at the sloppy remains of his Texas BBQ brisket. "A stud-for-hire."

Zen is obviously smart, and he has a winning personality. He looks physically fit. He may not have the strength to split logs but he could certainly stack them after someone like Ram did it for him. And finally, at the risk of sounding inappropriate, his face is very nice to look at. Especially when his cheeks are dimpling just so. I don't understand how he would be considered not good enough. Not that I approve of any of this business, mind you.

"Insufficient verticality," Zen explains, holding his hand about six inches over his head. "No one pays to bump with a guy who's five foot seven and a half." He drops his hand and points it straight at me. "Now I know what you're thinking: *Why don't you dose some pharma-grade HGH?*"

"That's not what I was thinking at all," I interrupt. "And what's HGH?"

"Human Growth Hormone. Anyway, lots of shorties have pumped themselves up with HGH to make themselves more sellable to RePro Reps. But you know what's happening? Users report that the increase in height is inversely proportional to a decrease in IQ! Ha! So these needle-happy juiceheads pass the test for verticality, but fail the minimum standards for intelligence!"

I'm able to understand approximately one in every five or so words that come out of Zen's mouth.

"And it also makes their stiffies shrink," he says, holding up a pinkie.

That much I can understand. And I wish I hadn't!

"Unless someone develops HGH that pumps up brains *and* bodies, I'm only good enough for everythingbut. Doomed to be a Worm, never a Sperm."

"'I am a worm, not a man,'" I recite by memory. "'Scorned by man, despised by the people.'"

"Yes!" Zen says, his face alight. "That's how I feel sometimes!"

"Christ said it when he was under persecution," I explain.

"He did, did He?" Zen says bemusedly, shaking his head at me. "You make a really great witness for Goodside, Harmony."

I think this is a compliment, so I accept it. "Thank you."

"But you still have a lot to learn about life on this side of the gates."

Zen is right. I do have a lot to learn. Othersiders rumormonger about the willful unknowingness of the Church, but God has placed in the human heart a desire to know the Truth. The more I know about Melody's decision to turn pro, the easier it will be for me to show her that earthly riches can't compare to Heaven's rewards.

Then maybe, just maybe, we can take the right path together.

Zen searches through his pockets, then hands me what looks like a debit card.

"What's this?" I ask.

"It's a Lost-and-Found card, for emergencies. It works even if you're not on the MiNet. If you get lost, just finger-swipe right here," he says, pointing to a small X marking the spot, "and I get an alert to find you, wherever you are."

I clutch the card in my hand. "Why would you give this to me?"

"Oh, it's no big," Zen says. "My parents gave me a bunch of them after all the floods and earthquakes. I figure that you're new to Otherside and might wind up somewhere you didn't mean to go. . . ."

His kindness brings tears to my eyes.

"What I meant was, why would you want to help *me*?"

He shrugs. "Helping people is kind of my hobby."

I look down at the card once more. "But you don't even know me. . . ."

Zen shakes his head as if the answer is obvious.

"You're Melody's sister, Harmony. We'll know each other for the rest of our lives."

SECOND

A free society cannot force girls to have children, but a free market can richly reward those who do.

—Ashley and Tyler Mayflower, PhDs,
Princeton University

harmony
melody

I WAKE AT DAWN IN PANIC, NOT PRAYER.

Who am I? Where am I? Why am I here?

I'm on the floor, soaked with sweat, blankets twisted around my legs like invasive vines choking the tomato plants.

Why am I not in my bunk?

Where are Laura, Katie, and Emily?

I'm about to cry out when a lump on the bed next to me rolls over, smacks her lips together, and sighs. That's when I remember:

The sighing lump is Melody.

I'm on the floor of her room.

She's my sister.

She's my twin.

Melody mumbles a word I can't quite make out. And even if I could, I probably wouldn't understand what it means. She was studying her advanced biogenetics flex-book when I came in to say good night. She said her parents make her read her most challenging subjects before bedtime.

"Even my dreams are educational," she said. "I never get a rest, not even when I'm asleep."

I read the Scripture every evening. Is that why I dream of Jesus?

Almost immediately the guilt of being here instead of where I should be settles heavy upon me. I make up for the omission with a morning offering.

"'Let the morning bring me word of your unfailing love,'" I whisper, so as not to disturb Melody. "'For I have put my trust in you. Show me the way I should go, for to you I lift up my soul.'"

A good psalm usually sets me right. But I'm feeling particularly out of sorts this morning. I unwind the blankets from my legs, gather up my pillow, and tiptoe out of Melody's bedroom. I feel my way down the dim hall back into the guest room where I had started out the night.

When I got back to the house yesterday, my suitcase wasn't on the doorstep as I had feared. But Melody wasn't there to welcome me either, as I had hoped. The front door was locked but I didn't panic because I heard noises coming from the backyard, a *fwoop fwoop fwoop*ing that sounded mechanical but I could in no other way identify.

I made my way around back and found Melody in the backyard defending a soccer goal from a machine launching one ball (*fwoop*) after another (*fwoop fwoop*) at unpredictable angles and terrifying speed. I flinched with every *fwoop*. Melody jumped and lunged and caught each black-and-white blur with just enough time to toss it to the side before the next *fwoop* hurtled straight for her. She never stopped moving. Dozens of soccer balls rolled onto the grass, but not a single ball slipped past her fingertips and inside the goal.

Only after the final *fwoop* did Melody allow herself to bend over, rest her hands on her knees, and gulp for air.

"How long have you been standing there?"

"Just a few minutes," I replied. "How long have you been practicing?"

"Long enough so my parents won't get pissy about not practicing long enough."

I nervously patted the netting on my veil.

"Did Zen help you pick that out?" she asked.

"No," I replied. "This is the same one I was wearing earlier. I didn't buy one after all."

"Oh."

Then she picked up one of the balls and started bouncing it from one knee to the other. She seemed worried about something, but I was reluctant to ask what it was. I was afraid to say or do anything that might result in her asking me to leave and never come back.

"That's okay," I said, unclipping my veil from my scalp

and shaking out my hair. "It's a relief to take it off, to tell you the truth."

She let the ball drop to the ground and gestured for me to follow her inside.

"I moved your suitcase into the guest room so you can change into something more comfortable in there."

"Thank you."

Melody opened the door to the room in which I would be staying, and gestured up to the patchwork of pressed tin tiles in the ceiling, then down to a puzzle of dark and light, long and short wood planks in the floor.

"My parents recycled the whole house. It's totally green."

She paused, then waited for me to say something, so I did.

"That's interesting."

"I know it's not exactly the nature you're used to," Melody said, touching her hand to the brass doorknob. "But it's as all natural as you can get off the farm."

I realized then that she was trying her best to find common ground, to make me feel welcome in her home. I wanted to embrace her to thank her for her compassion before she closed the door behind her. But I didn't. I was afraid such a display might provoke a sudden change of heart.

This guest room is roughly the same size as the room I share with Laura, Katie, and Emily. But with just one bed in the middle of the room, it feels far more spacious than any room I've ever slept in. That's why I crept into Melody's room in the middle of the night and slept near her on the floor. I've never slept alone. I'm too used to falling asleep to the rise and fall of peaceful breathing. I knew I'd toss and turn all night in the silence.

"Melllooooooodeee? Helloooooooo . . . ?"

Oh my grace! I jump at the sound of a voice coming from the front of the house. It sounds too low to be a woman, but too high to be a man. Who is it? How did he/she get in the house?

"Let me see yoooooooooou."

I don't know who would be visiting Melody at this early hour, but I rush toward the front door to find out. I freeze when I reach the common room.

"I've got the BEST NEWS, Miss Melody Mayflower!"

The voice isn't coming from a visitor. It's coming from a man projected larger than life-size on the MiVu wall. It's almost impossible to notice anything about him other than his suit, which is illuminated with electrified stripes of red, orange, yellow, green, blue, indigo, and violet.

"I want to see the look on your face when I tell yooooooooou." He trills the last word, reminding me of a soprano who holds her notes just a beat longer than everyone else in the Church choir.

I timidly approach the screen. The first thing I do is lower the volume. This man's voice carries and I don't want him waking up Melody. There's a box lit up in lower right-hand corner indicating that MiVu is in 1Vu mode right now. There are two more boxes that are blinking questions: 2Vu? 2Vu? 2Vu? Or: @Vu? @Vu? @Vu? We don't have MiVu in Goodside, so I'm not too familiar with the technology, but I believe "2Vu" means we can only see each other. And "@Vu" means that we can be seen by anyone who is plugged into the system right now who wants to see us. As I consider which box to press, the man on the screen keeps up his one-sided conversation.

"Whoopsie! What time is it there? It's nearly lunchtime here in Stockholm. This scouting trip has been UH. MAZE. ING. I was just saying to myself, *Lib. Have you ever seen so many blond, blue-eyed hunkaspunks in your WHOLE LIFE?* And myself replied, *No, Lib. I have not.*"

Lib. I rack my brains trying to remember who Lib is. I know Melody has mentioned him, but I can't remember. . . .

"There's one fine speci*man* I was all ready to introduce to the Jaydens. . . ."

Now I remember! Lib is Melody's Reproductive Representative! He's the one who recruited her to be a Surrogette! Melody said he was a colorful character, but I hadn't expected him to wear a suit that glows like an electric rainbow. Maybe I can tell him that Melody has had a change of heart. She doesn't want to be a Surrogette after all. Would he believe me? Of course then I would have to do some prayerful witnessing to make Melody believe it herself.

"GUESS WHAT?"

I press the 2Vu option.

"Hey gorgeous! You ARE there!" Lib crows when I come into his Vu. "Like the lumina suit?" he asks, stretching out to get a full view of the electric rainbow running up and down his arms. When I respond with a wince, he sighs, then presses a button on his wrist to make the lights go out. "It's a bit too much first thing in the morning, isn't it?"

Now that I get a better look, I see that Lib is bald, save for a silvery inch-wide strip of hair running front to back across his scalp. His skin is as brown as an acorn, and his face is stretched taut and unlined, as is often seen in older men of means in Otherside. Even the skin in his eye sockets is pulled tight, making them bulge in surprise at all times. Those lavender eyes are scrolling up down and all around as he takes in my appearance as carefully as I am taking in his. Usually this would make me feel uncomfortable, but something about Lib tells me that he's not looking at me with impure interest.

"You got some SUN! It gives you that FRESH, OUT-DOORSY look!"

It becomes clear that Lib uses his expressive voice to overcompensate for his frozen face. He drops it to a conspiratorial whisper, beckons for me to come closer to the screen.

"Just don't get too much. A little rosy glow is okay, you just don't want to get . . . ah, too dark. That's not what the Jaydens hired you for. They don't give a hoot about the multiculti trends! They are SO into Euro! That milky

71

complexion is one of your greatest assets."

Oh! He thinks I'm Melody! She must not have told Lib that I'm staying with her for a while. I'm about to reveal myself as the twin sister, but he doesn't stop talking long enough to give me the chance.

"And while we're talking superficials, that . . . that . . . THING you're wearing is so TERMINAL and so FERTILICIOUS at the same time."

I look down at my long white cotton nightdress.

"You are so smart to cover up as much skin as possible," Lib continues with admiration in his voice. "I've been selling everyone since you signed with me: MELODY MAYFLOWER IS THE FULL PACKAGE. Beauty and brains. I wish all my clients were as bright as you."

I try to correct his mistake. "Actually, I'm not—"

"Oh, but you ARE. You must spend most your day fending off amateur offers from all the . . ." He screws up his mouth, just about the only part of his face he can move. "*Opportunistic humpers* at your high school."

"But—"

"Do you have ANY IDEA how many of my clients break their conception contracts? They have NO appreciation for all the hard work I put in to making the perfect three-way match." He snorts. "TOO HORMONAL to think about how their choices affect their OWN futures."

"Mr. Lib, sir, I—"

"They all prooooooomise to keep it pure. They're all like"—his voice gets higher—"*Lib! I won't bump with him! He's my everythingbut!* Then they do a little too much TOCIN DOSIN' and the next thing I know these girls have forgotten the *but* in *everythingbut* and they're BUMP-ING with some unaccredited"—he turns his head and sticks out his tongue—"*WORM.*"

Worm. That's how Zen referred to himself yesterday.

"I'm sorry," Lib says with a sniff. "I'm just SO EMO-TIONAL today. Becaaaaaaaaause . . ." He makes a strange choking noise, then covers his mouth with his hands as if he's unsure whether he's capable of delivering his message after all. Then he opens up his hands to make a mega-phone. "YOU'RE GONNA GET BUMPED BY THE BEST MAN BRAND IN THE BUSINESS."

His words push me backward onto the couch, a sight that makes Lib cackle and clap with delight.

"W-w-what?"

"And you're not gonna BELIEVE who it is. I still can't believe it myself."

I can't believe any of this.

"I've got one word for you." He closes his eyes, takes a breath, then says with reverential solemnity, "Jondoe."

This word means nothing to me but it means every-thing to Lib.

"ARE YOU TERMINATED? BECAUSE I AM BEYOND TERMINATED."

I think I might be terminated and I don't even know what he is talking about.

"Jondoe," Lib keeps saying to himself. "Jondoe. When

73

the Mrs. finally convinced the Mr. to go commercial, I never dreamed their application would be approved by the all-time highest scorer on the Standards. Believe the hype! He's got the fastest, strongest swimmers ever recorded!" Lib mops the sweat off his forehead with his sleeve. "He's got a perfect five-star ranking among triple-platinum-level customers who have employed his services. Ash and Ty will TERMINATE when you tell them that!" Then Lib does his best to twist his frozen face into a look of exaggerated concern. "Oh, sweetie! You're IN SHOCK."

This, I understand. I *am* in shock. She's been waiting for this news for years. It certainly complicates my plans to get Melody to get married and live with me and Ram in faith and fellowship as all good and obedient Church girls should.

Lib leans in and cups his mouth with one hand to share a secret, and I instinctively come closer to hear it.

"I. EXIST. FOR. YOU," he says. "I live for *you* and I die for *you*."

I object to such Christlike claims coming from a sinner's mouth, but can't raise my voice in protest.

"You know to what *great lengths* I went to make sure your file was *flawless*," he says in an emphatic whisper. "I put my *reputation* on the line for you. I *pulled strings*. I called in *favors*. Let's just put it this way, Miss Melody Mayflower, I *earned* my fifteen percent!" He wipes his immobile brow, sits back, and raises the volume. "And it worked! It's a testament to all my hard work that Jondoe accepted the

Jaydens' bid. He's very selective, he takes only a fraction of the offers that come along. You can tell Ash and Ty that getting into the number one college in the WORLD will be a no-brainer after *Jondoe* gets into *you!*"

He cackles wildly.

"I cannot thank you enough for all your efforts in keeping your EYES on the PURITY PRIZE." He traces an imaginary line from my neck to my ankles. "Never in my wildest dreams did I think that you would have the opportunity to bump with Jondoe." His eyes are tearing up, the only visible sign on his face that he's overcome with emotion. "From what we've all seen and heard about Jondoe, he'll be WORTH EVERY MICROSECOND of frustrated restraint. . . ." He rubs his palms together with relish.

My sister is still chaste. It's not too late to protect that gift of purity, but I need to intervene right now, to tell Lib that I will endure fire raining down from Heaven before I will allow my sister to prostitute herself for procreation and profit. The best investment she can make is in God. If only Lib devoted as much time and energy into glorifying the Lord as he put into his immoral business, he too would be saved.

"I can see your heart pounding!"

I clutch my chest to feel what Lib can see. This is my chance to find my voice. To tell Lib I'm not who he thinks I am, nor is my sister. I must coax the words out of my throat. I can't let fear stop me. Being scared means that I trust my own feelings more than I trust God, and that's just disrespectful.

"Where are you in your cycle? Oh, WHO CARES? Let's get you two BUMPING right away. We don't want another trimester to go by with a FLAT TUMMY. And not to put any pressure on you or anything, but it would be just BREEDY if you could deliver the goods by next March. The Jaydens have an interest in zodiacology. Remember how I negotiated that bonus for delivering a Pisces? Another stroke of BRILLLLLLIANCE!"

I clear my throat. "Excuse me," I say more firmly, but he talks right over me.

"Let me put you in the mood! I've got his most recent Tocin ad right here! Prepare to be dazzled! Are you ready to be dazzled?"

"But I'm not Mel—"

"I mean it! You must prepare yourself right now!"

Lib disappears and in the very next moment . . .

"Behold the most BEAUTIFUL sight you have ever seen!"

"But—ohhhhh . . ."

This is a transcendent understatement.

"That flowing, golden hair . . ." Lib raves from a reduced screen in the corner. "Those soulful brown eyes . . ."

I am basking in the true light of the Alpha and Omega.

"No need for a dose of Tocin to OPEN YOU UP to this one! Look at him!"

I do.
And
I
am
reborn.

melody
harmony

I THINK HARMONY MISSES GOODSIDE ALREADY. SHE'S BEYOND wanked this morning. I mean, for *her*. Yesterday she couldn't wait to go out and faith hard in the face of non-believers at the Mallplex. But today she's content to stay in while I'm at school.

When Harmony first told me that she'd changed her mind about tagging along, I was for seriously relieved because I didn't know how I was going to break the news that she could in no way come with me to school today. We're all supposed to stop stressing about opposing belief systems because we're more, like, mature now and stuff. But guess what? The Churchies still freak everyone out. Not too long ago some Churchies from a local settlement took over Palmer Square and asked me, Malia, and Shoko if we had God when all we wanted to do was buy retro froyo. Then we all joked about how their godfreakiness could infect us and turn us from totally normal to totally not. And for days, even weeks afterward, the three of us laughed about it, like, "Ha. I'm going to burn in hell. Ha. Ha. Ha." But the jokes are never really all that funny.

Letting Harmony come to school with me on a regular day would be bad enough, but today it would be terminal. It's a big day for me with the Pro/Am vote and all. Ventura Vida poses enough of a challenge as it is. I don't need my secret identical twin stalking around the halls asking everyone if they have God.

Harmony was so calm and focused yesterday, remarkably so considering how jarring it must have been to leave Goodside behind. Since I found her on her knees in the common room this morning, however, she's been acting kind of blinky. It's possible she always wakes up like this. Maybe she's got undiagnosed ADHD and she needs to self-medicate by, like, milking a cow or something to calm down. But I have a feeling she's unnerved by something, or rather, someone else entirely.

"Hey. Did Zen say something . . . ?"

For all I know, he could've brought up our ridiculous "contract" and tried to persuade Harmony to proxy pregg on my behalf. When she doesn't answer I repeat the question, assuming she can't hear me over the cracklesnap of bubbling batter in a frying pan I didn't even know we owned.

"Who?" Harmony asks, without turning away from the stove.

"Zen."

"Zen?"

"Yes, Zen," I say, growing impatient, "The boy you met yesterday . . ."

She turns, a flicker of recognition crossing her face as she comes toward me with a steaming pancake balanced on a spatula. "Oh, *Zen*," she says in an airy, distracted way.

"Yes, *Zen*," I say in a tone that matches hers note for note. "Did he say or *do* something . . . um, *inappropriate* yesterday?"

"What?" Harmony clumsily flips the pancake half on, half off my plate. When she boosts it back onto the plate with the spatula, it breaks in half. "Oops. Sorry."

I'm trying not to lose it, but she is not making it easy. *"Did Zen say or do something inappropriate yesterday?"*

"Ohhhh . . ." she says, as if checking in to the conversation for the first time. "No."

When she doesn't elaborate, I do. "Because you're acting kind of . . ." I choose the next word carefully. *"Different* today."

"I am?" she asks, a note of worry in her voice. "I guess I'm worn out from yesterday. It's a lot to take in all at once."

I imagine that this is true. I barely know her, and yet I can't let go of the feeling that there's something *off* about her behavior this morning. But I don't think I'll get much out of her with repeated prodding.

"Well," I reply, deciding to keep it light. "You already make your way around this kitchen better than I do."

It's actually pretty funny seeing Harmony bustle around our kitchen. Ash and Ty know I'll never be bothered to nuke a freezerful of instant meals, so they provide me with a per diem for takeout whenever they're away. Watching Harmony put together a fine breakfast out of some eggs and left-behinds in our pantry, I get a glimpse of an alternate destiny. I see what I would've looked like if *I* were the one trained in the domestic arts to make a good wife at sixteen. (Or, as Harmony's starter engagement would have had it, thirteen.)

She brushes a strand of hair out of her clear blue eyes. *They're pretty,* I think, before remembering, *Oh, yeah. They're just like mine.*

"If you didn't buy a new veil, what did you and Zen do alone together for three hours?"

Funny how Zen has had zero time for me, and yet had all afternoon for Harmony.

"We went to Plain & Simple to shop for a new veil, but I didn't buy one," she says as she briskly mixes more batter. "They were all too expensive and . . ." Her voice trails off and her hand spins even more vigorously around the inside of the bowl.

"And what?" I ask.

"And then we got some dinner at the U.S. Buff-A. Have you been there?"

I try not to shoot her a condescending look. I remind myself that the U.S. Buff-A has yet to open a franchise in Goodside. I smile and nod instead.

"Zen warned me that the Maine lobster-roll appetizer wouldn't go well with the Pennsylvania cheesesteak," she says, clutching her stomach and sticking out her tongue. "But I didn't listen. . . ."

I take the final bite from my first pancake before reaching for my second. Harmony hasn't eaten a thing.

"Did you meet anyone else while you were there?"

Harmony doesn't stop stirring. "No. Zen blinded his MiNet so we could have some privacy."

Of course he did. How gentlemanly of him.

"So what did you talk about?"

"You." She stops mixing and levels her gaze at me. "Zen cares about you."

"Zen cares about everyone. It's, like, his thing."

It's almost pathological, really, his need to help people. This is why *he's* the go-to guy for driving home a bunch of wasted Cheerclones after their orgy. Gah.

"Maybe," Harmony says. "But he *really* cares about you. It's too bad about his insufficient verticality."

I choke on my pancake, coughing a puff of flour across the countertop.

"Then you wouldn't have to share yourself with someone you've never even met."

Then she picks up a sponge and cleans up the mess I just made.

82

I'm still thwacking my chest with the heel of my palm, trying to dislodge a wad of unchewed dough. I have no time to offer my rebuttal because I'm interrupted by an all-too-familiar annoyance coming from the MiVu.

"Wake up, Pell-Mel! Wakey-wakey!"

"Oh!" Harmony jumps, splattering a spoonful of batter across her nightgown.

"It's just Ash and Ty," I croak. "Right on time for their a.m. stalking."

Every school day at seven a.m., my parents shout at me until I turn on the 2Vu to confirm I'm keeping myself alive in their absence.

"PELL-MEL. PELL-MEL. PELL-MEL." So goes the chant in the other room.

"If I don't respond within two minutes, they call 911."

"It's nice that they care," Harmony says.

"Yeah," I snort. "That's one way of looking at it."

Between the wake-up calls, the 24/7 stalk app, and the GUARDIAN (Guaranteed Under-Age Remote Detection of Illegal Alcohol and Narcotics) monitor, my parents are far more oppressive when they're on the other side of the world than when they're right down the hall.

When Harmony makes a move with me toward the common room, I suggest that she stay in the kitchen instead.

"Don't you want them to meet me?" she asks, a wounded expression on her face.

"I do," I say. "Just not right now." This is true. I barely

have the time or energy to deal with the standard-issue Ash and Ty interrogation. I know I can't handle a grilling over the one girl in the world who could do *the* most damage to my uniqueness quotient.

"They know about me . . . right?" she asks in a fragile voice.

"*Of course* they know about you."

From the look of relief on her face, it's clear that she interprets the "of course" as proof of the value I place on our relationship.

I don't have the heart to tell her that "of course" has nothing to do with me and everything to do with my parents' "no secrets" policy, or that they came to find out about her as they discover most things: through high-tech surveillance. After they tracked my MiChat minutes and freaked out about all the incoming calls from Goodside, they jumped to ludicrous conclusions and confronted me with the "evidence" in their usual tag-teaming style.

"We won't stand back and let you run off with a Church boy!" warned Ash.

"We didn't prep you for all these years to lose you to a quiverfilling cult!" snapped Ty.

They were for seriously convinced that I'd fallen in with the evangelical crowd as an exercise in teen rebellion. Their accusations were so off-the-spring crazy that I hoped the truth—that I had been found by my identical twin sister raised by Churchies in Goodside—would strike them almost as anticlimactic by comparison. I was, of course, wrong. They didn't ask a single question as to the impact such an astounding discovery would have on me *emotionally*, but immediately started debating the impact Harmony could have on me *financially*.

"You're *certain* she's not on the market," Ash said.

"She's engaged to be married," I assured them.

"She could counterfeit and undercut you," Ty coldly pointed out.

"It's against her religion," I told them.

My parents made me promise to limit my contact with Harmony until after I bumped, which, you know, should be any day now. And I did. Or I tried to anyway. Until she showed up on my doorstep.

Harmony's very existence has the potential to raise too many questions about my family history, a mysterious mess that Lib has taken it upon himself, as my RePro Rep, to handle with the utmost skill. And only when absolutely necessary, *sketchiness*. Gah. If Lib knew Harmony was here he'd drop dead on the spot. And if he knew I'd taken her to the Meadowlands Mallplex yesterday and that she was flipping pancakes in my kitchen at this moment, he'd raise himself up from the grave just for the satisfaction of dropping dead again. He loves drama, but not when it gets in the way of business.

Meanwhile Harmony is unaware of the havoc she's wreaked, first by contacting me, and again by coming to stay. She seems pretty much oblivious to just about everything right now, as she smiles into space and dreamily traces her fingers along the sticky batter spiderwebbing across her nightshirt. Why didn't I blind her chats? Why didn't I make her go back yesterday?

Unfortunately, my parents already know more about her than I'd like them to. So as I stride toward the MiVu, I decide that all I can do is try to keep their meddling to a minimum at the moment, just long enough to get me through this day.

Ash and Ty are now arguing to themselves about whether they've given me enough time to respond or should they just dial 911 right now. For all the money my parents have shelled out on the latest in teen-tracking technologies, they don't seem to trust any of it.

"I'm alive," I announce to my parents as I sweep into their 2Vu. "Just like the stalk app says I am."

Ash and Ty are fit and attractive blue-eyed blonds, like me. From looks alone, I could totally pass as their own, but they've always gone out of their way to tell people I'm adopted. They knew the Virus would make this the likeliest parental model of the future, and have always held me up as the prime example of what could be achieved when nature's gifts are nurtured to perfection.

Not *too* much pressure, right?

Ash speaks first. She usually does.

"How *are* you?"

I clench. My parents never, ever begin a conversation by asking such a question. No, they begin all conversations by offering constructive criticism and pointing out all ways I'm not living up to my file. A more typical greeting would have been:

"You almost let two balls slip past you yesterday, sweetie."

"You didn't practice your guitar all week. You know the arts are the weakest part of your profile, and with a name like Melody . . ."

My parents were professors at the University until I signed my conception contract eighteen months ago. That's when they reminded me that they were both in their forties, which put them, statistically speaking, more than halfway to their deaths. This was just totally unacceptable because there was just so much of life they hadn't lived, so much stuff they had never gotten around to doing because they were too busy schooling, working, and, since they adopted me sixteen years earlier, prepping me to be the well-rounded and highly sought-after Surrogette they always knew I would become. Rarely were they themselves the ones instructing me in the fine art of gene splicing or eyeliner application, but all that expert outsourcing doesn't just happen by itself, does it?

Their investment in me paid off. Literally. Thanks to the generous six-figure signing bonus Lib got out of the Jaydens, they're now out there *living life*, which includes doing all that undone stuff like walking the Great Wall of China and learning the didgeridoo from Australian aborigines. They claim that it's all material for some great research project in progress, but I highly doubt it.

"Any word from Lib lately, honey?" they ask now in unison.

"Um, no. Why?" I ask.

My parents grin and grip each other's hands.

"Because we met an *awesome* couple on safari. They have a son your age," says Ash.

I don't like where this is headed.

"And they also have an older daughter who is *desperate* for a Surrogette," she continues.

"You should be that Surrogette," says Ty.

My parents are nothing if not direct. My mouth hangs open.

"Our friends are *loaded*, Melody," adds Ty. "We can cut out the middleman and save ourselves fifteen percent."

I'm beyond shocked. My deal with the Jaydens was their crowing achievement as parents. Why would they even consider messing it up?

"My contract . . ." I can barely speak.

"We're afraid you're wasting your reproductivity," says Ash.

"With all this waiting around," says Ty.

I've told them to lay off the Tocin. They are totally dosed. That's the only explanation.

"Hahahahaha. You got me, guys."

I'm the only one laughing. I can tell from their tight, downturned mouths that they are dead serious. They're starting to scare me.

"Here's the thing, Melody," Ash begins.

And that's when they tell me that it's not about the money that they spent and don't have anymore, it's the money they spent that they *never* had.

"We borrowed against the equity on your Eggs."

I cannot believe what I'm hearing.

"YOU *WHAT*?"

Harmony yelps quietly. I surprise even myself with the outburst.

I barely hear what they say next, but what I do hear is bad enough.

My parents had my reproductive potential appraised when I was eleven, before I even signed on with Lib. Then they took out a five-year Egg Equity loan, which basically means that they borrowed against my projected future earnings as a Surrogette. They put that capital toward the strategic development of my most marketable traits and talents.

"How do you think we could afford to send you to that soccer training clinic in Brazil?"

"Or guitar lessons with a Grammy winner?"

"You think the Global U. summer camp comes cheap?"

This strategic reinvestment in my brand, they believed, would up my market value and put me well over the original appraisal. And when the Jaydens' bid came in so strong, it looked like I would definitely earn back everything they had borrowed and more. There was just one problem with their plan.

"You should have delivered by now," says Ash.

"You should be finishing up your second contract and considering a third," says Ty.

They were banking that I'd deliver *three* times before my obsolescence?

"But you're not."

"And it's time to pay that money back."

How could they let this happen? How could they have turned their only daughter into a toxic asset in need of a quick bump bailout? I expected more from them. If not as parents, then as *economists*.

"You're still young!" says Ash with an edge to her voice.

"You can pregg with our new friends," says Ty, eerily matching her tone, "and *still* have time left to deliver for the Jaydens."

I can't listen for another microsecond. I wink and blink and make them vanish from the MiVu without a word.

Now I'm shaking from the inside out. I take a deep, calming breath and repeat the words my positive energist taught me to say when I've got a problem and don't know how to solve it.

I am smart.

I am stunning.

I am strong.

I am everything I need to be.

Hopefully the money they spent putting me *in* this crisis helped me develop the skills to get myself *out* of it.

"Do you want to talk about what just happened?"

Harmony has changed into a button-front dress that is plainer than the one she wore yesterday, tinged yellow, and slightly shorter too, a scandalous ankle length. Her gloves stop at the wrists. This must be the Church version of casual wear.

"No," I reply. "There's nothing to discuss."

"But—"

"Honor thy parents is one of *your* commandments. Honor thy contracts is one of mine." I try to say it like I mean it. "I'm *not* a renegger."

"So you're okay?"

I nod vigorously, afraid that my voice might betray my lack of confidence.

Harmony fusses with her gloves for a moment, then says, "Amen to that."

And if I were the praying kind, I just might have amened along with her.

harmony
melody

I'M SITTING ON THE FLOOR IN THE MIDDLE OF MELODY'S closet, averting my eyes as she models yet another outfit in front of the mirror.

"How does this look?" she asks, more to the mirror than to me.

Those second-skin jeans and Co-Ed Naked Human Evolution League T-shirt don't look any different from any of the other combinations of clothing she's put on and taken off in the past ten minutes: *sacrilegious*. But then I remind myself that here in Otherside, such provocative outfits aren't against the Orders. If I'm going to blend in here, I need to pay close attention to how such fashions are put together.

"Is this an outfit that says, *I'll be bumped any day now?*"

When she turns to look at me, I realize that she's waiting for my opinion.

"Y-y-yes?"

She slaps her hand to her forehead. "Look who I'm asking!" She gestures at my full-skirted day dress and matching gloves. "I bet you never worry about what to wear."

When I realize that she's being playful, not judgmental, I return her smile. "By dressing simply and humbly, we don't waste time worrying about our appearance. We have more time to serve God and our community."

"I wonder how much more I could accomplish," Melody says, throwing the T aside and reaching for a gauzy floral blouse, "if I didn't go through this every single day."

I think about my big housesisters, Mary, Lucy, and Annie, and it makes me giggle to imagine them agonizing over whether to wear the pink day dress or the *other* pink day dress, blue or blue. Even my little housesisters, Laura, Katie, and Emily, don't dither over which shade of white they'll wear today. They've been awake for two hours already, have already done their outdoor chores (gathering eggs, milking cows, collecting wood for the fire) and indoor chores (setting the table, serving the meal, clearing up) and are now gathering for the Monday-morning prayershare. This is the first one I've missed since I was struck down by mule flu last year. Forgive me for saying so, but I don't regret not being there.

Please don't think I'm disrespecting the power of

fellowship and group prayer. When we join together in worship, we gain one another's strength. However, we've been taught that we can only ask for things that bring glory to God and I don't see how it glorifies God when Laura asks Him to cure her bad breath. He's all the way up in Heaven and not sharing the same loom. She's wasting God's time.

It pains me to say this, but Katie uses prayershare to shed embarrassing light on others' failings under the pretense of saving a soul. For example, a few weeks ago she said, "Please pray for my friend who has lust in her heart for her fiancé's brother." And nobody could pray hard for the rest of the session because we were too busy not so quietly speculating who in our prayerclique had lust in her heart for her future brother-in-law. Such gossip isn't praiseworthy. And it was doubly pointless because everyone already knows that Emily sobbed for a week after she was betrothed in her Blooming to the younger, bucktoothed Stoltzfus boy.

"Thanks for cleaning up."

Without even realizing it, I have gathered up all of Melody's T-shirts and folded them neatly in a stack. The one on top is printed with an image of a green pill on a wet pink tongue with the words OPEN UP WITH TOCIN. I instinctively turn it over to the blank side.

"So. What do you think?"

I look up to see that Melody has changed into a silky sleeveless T in a beautiful sky blue hue that I'm forbidden to wear unless—I mean, *until*—I give birth to a son.

"I like the flowery one better," I say, thinking quickly. "It's more . . . *maternal*."

"Maternal as in 'ready to bump.' Right?"

"Right," I reply, this time without a stammer.

Melody sighs as she puts the other blouse back on, assesses herself in the mirror once more. A look of triumph lights up her face. "Now, a last check on my hair and makeup!" she says as she runs out of the closet.

I don't follow her.

Instead, I pick up the blue shirt from the floor. The fabric is unlike anything I've ever felt before, virtually weightless, and so unlike the rough-hewn cotton and wool we use to make most of our clothing. I hold it up to marvel at the lack of discernible seams or stitches, clearly the product of neither spindle nor loom.

Melody bursts back into the closet. "Oh! I almost forgot!"

I yelp and drop the offensive shirt to the floor. Did she see me? No, she's too busy searching for something in her jewelry box. She holds what's she's looking for—a chain with a single, small bead—and regards it with a frown before putting it around her neck.

"So you'll be okay by yourself?" By the way she's blinking and rolling her eyes, I can tell that she's more focused on the MiNet than me.

I pray I won't be by myself for long.

"I don't have time to set up the touchpad for the MiNet

right now, so you won't be able to—"

"Oh, that's fine," I interrupt. "There's plenty in here"—I tap my Bible—"to keep me busy!"

"Um," she says distractedly, eyes racing in their sockets. "Right." Her eyes focus on the middle distance between us. "I'm leaving so . . . if you need . . ." More eye rolling. "Zen's *here*?" Without finishing her thought, she backs out of the closet in haste. A few moments later I hear the front door open and slam behind her. She doesn't say goodbye.

With fourteen housebrothers and housesisters, I'm rarely by myself. I like to go on long walks in the overgrown fields once cleared out for another never-built neighborhood. Ma still sees me as the sickly baby I once was and worries that I'll put too much stress on my delicate constitution. Going on those walks isn't against the Orders but is still a form of disobedience. I've always known my mother disapproves, but I've gone anyway. Not for the exercise, fresh air, or scenery. Just to be alone with my thoughts.

I pray I'll be forgiven for the worry I'm putting Ma through right now.

I shyly reclaim the blue T, then nervously hold it up to my own body, partly expecting to be discovered by several pairs of watching eyes all ready to chastise me for my transgressive ways. When it doesn't happen, I am emboldened to walk to the other side of the closet, where Melody's jeans are organized by color in tidy rows. I select silver.

The silence inside the closet is unnerving. I sing to

myself just to make some noise.

"You're knocked up . . ."

I bury my blushing face into my hands. Assimilating with the sinners is not going to be easy.

I have to remind myself that nothing I do here is against the Orders.

Cling to your faith in Christ, and keep your conscience clear.

I turn away from the mirror and unbutton my dress. Quickly, and still afraid of being scrutinized by invisible eyes, I pull on the jeans and slip on the T-shirt and . . . I still feel naked! The fabric is as light as air, no more than a whisper against my skin. It's indescribably strange to be covered up and yet, so . . . free. I cautiously look in the mirror, afraid that this is somehow a trick. . . .

That pretty girl in the mirror, openmouthed and pink in the cheeks, looks almost like an Othersider. There's just one minor adjustment.

The gloves come off.

Now she stands here in a T-shirt that brings out the blue in her eyes, and jeans that cling to every inch, two gloveless, ringless hands on her hips. This girl isn't Melody, though she looks exactly like Melody.

She is me.

melody
harmony

ZEN IS STRADDLING HIS BIKE IN MY DRIVEWAY.

"To what do I owe this great honor?" I ask, unlocking my own bike. "Are you here for me? Or are you and your new best friend shopping for chastity belts today?"

"I'm here to see *you*," he insists.

I wait for him to finish.

"To talk about *her*."

I knew it. I pull on my helmet and swing my leg over the crossbar.

"If you hadn't blinded your MiNet last night, you would know what I want to talk to you about."

"If *you* hadn't blinded your MiNet for the last *month*, you would know what I *don't* want to talk to you about."

"Look, I told you," he says, "I've got IAMs to study

for. Not everyone aces them the first time around."

A lot of good it's done me. My parents have already signed me up for another round because *near* perfect on the International Aptitude Measurements isn't perfect enough to get into Global U.

"I don't get why you're suddenly so obsessed with the IAMs anyway," I say, rolling my bike back and forth, crunching the gravel. "Weren't you the one telling me that brick-and-mortar institutions of higher learning are *so* last century? That my parents had the right idea, going out there and living life with the whole world as their classroom . . ."

I stop myself. My *awesome* parents are the last people I want to talk about right now. Gah. I change the subject.

"What did you say to Harmony yesterday?"

Zen looks relieved to return to this line of questioning.

"I said a lot of things," Zen says.

"You say whatever it takes to get everyone to like you."

He slumps over his handlebars and looks up at me with goo-gooey innocence. "Why do you think I'm always trying to get everyone to like me?"

"Zen! You *invented* the Like Me Algorithm!"

In ninth grade, Zen wrote an app that instantly cataloged the likes and dislikes of anyone who had ever created a MiNet profile and used that data to whatever ends he needed to get that person to like him.

"Not relevant," he says. "I never *used* it."

This is true. He destroyed the program immediately so it wouldn't be exploited by, in his words, "forces of evil."

"Your sister found me naturally charming. Just like you do."

I snort.

"In fact . . ." He throws his arms out in front of him as if presenting himself as a gift. "She might want me."

I make a big show out of laughing so hard I can hardly stand up.

"I'm serious!"

Still laughing, I push off down the hill.

"You're talking about a girl who thinks she'll go to hell if she shows a bit of ankle!" I yell into the breeze. "A person who wants me to marry one of her housebrothers at the end of the month."

"And why do you think that's so important to her?" he shouts from behind me.

"Maybe because she's been told her whole life that anyone who doesn't do things the Church way is going to burn in hell for all eternity? Because she's been brought up to believe that it's her mission in life to save as many of us sinners as possible? It would be a major failure if she couldn't even convince her own identical twin sister to have God."

"That's one way of seeing it," Zen says, struggling to keep up. He's got the better bike, but I've got longer, stronger legs. "I think *she's* the one who needs convincing, not you."

"And what did she say that makes you think that?"

"It wasn't what she said," Zen shouts. "It's what she *didn't* say. . . ."

Gah. Typical Zen.

"Promise me, Zen, you won't tell anyone at school about Harmony until I'm ready."

"Mel . . ."

"PROMISE OR I'LL TELL EVERYONE YOU STILL SLEEP WITH BOO BOO."

Boo Boo is Zen's girlbot. By sixteen years old, any self-respecting guy has replaced—or at least *supplemented*—his artificial lovin' with the real thing.

"We had good times together. I'm keeping her for sentimental reasons—"

"Oh, is *that* what they call it these days—"

"When you hit below the belt, you *really* hit below the belt—"

"JUST PROMISE."

"Okay." He rubs his helmet because he can't pull at the hair underneath. "I promise because I'm such a great friend, and *not* because I'm worried about anyone finding out about Boo Boo because guess what? It's common knowledge among dudes that we *all* hook up with our girlbots every now and again. . . ."

Gaaah. I pedal faster.

"Wait, Mel!" he says, panting harder now as I pick up the pace. "I'm being serious now. What if there's more than what Harmony is telling you . . . ?"

"I don't have time for your hypotheticals today!"

I zoom ahead, leaving him behind as if he's cemented to the sidewalk.

harmony
melody

NOW THAT MELODY IS GONE, ALL I HAVE TO DO IS WAIT.

"Do me a favor," Lib had said. "Skip school. Stay home today. Play NOOKY HOOKY. Because GUESS WHAT! It turns out our boy Jondoe was in New York City over the weekend to bump the mayor's daughter. She pregged on the first try! What a pro. Anyway, now he's got a few days free before he has to fly out to Los Angeles to promote his new fragrance. He can be there this AFTERNOON. Will you skip school so I can set up a one-on-one?"

I nodded mutely.

"THAT'S MY GIRL. I don't want another day to go by, Miss Melody Mayflower. Let's deliver what the Jaydens are SO WILLING to pay SO MUCH for. This is your FUTURE we're talking about." He stopped, assumed a more serious tone. "You do realize that your life is about to change."

My life already had.

"Once this news hits the MiNet, the optics are gonna go OFF THE SPRING. Your pregg will be famous. Morning sickness is NOTHING compared to how green with envy they'll be when they find out who's bumping you. . . ."

I didn't hear anything else Lib said. When he vanished from MiVu, taking my Morning Star with him, I fell to my knees, humbled by the task that God had put before me.

Lib believed that I was Melody—and it's his job to know everything about her. It shouldn't be too hard to lead a stranger into believing the same. I only have to pretend long enough to make him change his mind about . . . doing what he's supposed to do with my sister and, if possible, forsake his sinful profession altogether. If Jesus could spend His time preaching to the prostitutes, so can I.

Because I'm being challenged to serve a higher truth.

And saving Jondoe must be part of the plan now too.

melody
harmony

GAH. I HATE BIKING TO SCHOOL. BUT AS PRESIDENT OF THE ECOmmunity Club, my parents say I have to serve as a conscientious example.

I arrive at school all windswept and slightly sweaty, just in time to see Shoko clamber down the steps from the bus everyone calls the Bumpmobile. It provides rides to and from school for all students with certified pregnancies, no matter how close they live to campus. Malia, Shoko, and I used to bike together every day and rant about the Cheerclones who can't walk one-tenth of a mile to school but can still flip handsprings well into their third trimester.

"We're gonna rock big bellies on our bikes!" we used to brag. "We won't be like those lazy breeders taking the Bumpmobile."

Now Shoko sits next to those lazy breeders every morning swapping cures for stretch marks. Malia is in lockdown. And I bike to school alone.

I don't hold a grudge against Shoko. Really. She's been an awesome president. There's a lot of tension between amateurs and pros at school. Like, amateurs look down on pros for bumping with strangers, not boyfriends. Or they pity us for missing out on all the partner-swapping fun at the masSEX parties. And pros say amateurs are jealous because they aren't good enough to pregg for profit. And even if they were, they probably wouldn't have the will-power to keep their legs closed until it was time to fulfill their contractual obligations. That sort of cattiness threatened to end the Alliance before it even began. But as the rare amateur *turned* pro, Shoko has served as an inspiration and intermediary between both sides.

So that's the good news. The bad news is that this second pregg has given Shoko a major case of what experts call "adolescent amnio-amnesia." I swear she's dropped at least ten IQ points per trimester. She's at thirty-nine and a half weeks now and can't stay focused on anything. If she's carrying her third pregg in college, she'll fail out for serious. Like right now she waddles right past me without saying hello. As her peer birthcoach, the only nonrelative allowed in the delivery room, I'd be offended if I weren't so used to it.

I tap the bell to get her attention.

RING! RING! RING! "Shoko, hello!" *RING! RING! RING!*

"Oy!" she yelps, clutching her belly. "Don't break my water!"

She's joking. At least I think she's joking. Bounding off the bus right behind Shoko is none other than Ventura Vida. She and her adorable six-month bump believe otherwise.

"Oh, no!" she trills. "You rilly, rilly can't go into labor until after the vote!"

Ventura smiles with more gums than teeth. I guess she's figured out that she's prettier when she's meaner.

"Don't worry," Shoko says to Ventura and the group of variously pregnant girls surrounding her, many of whom I know from the Pro/Am. "I just know Burrito will take it to forty-two weeks, just like the first one."

"You've got a very *hospitable* womb," says Ventura, which makes everyone, including Shoko, laugh so hard that there must be more to it than what I'm hearing, the punch line for a joke that began on the bus.

"Ugh. I hope Sugar Booger doesn't go to forty-two weeks," groans Celine Lichtblau, who, in my opinion, needs to tell her OB to adjust the dose on her AntiTocin. Taken in the right amounts, AntiTocin counteracts the all-natural chemical bond between biomom and pregg. Too much AntiTocin makes you a cranky bitch for nine months straight.

Ventura hoists her cleavage to get attention. It works. Her bra started as an A minus and is currently a D plus. With her luck, by the time she pushes, she'll probably be a full F, the only time such a grade change can be considered progress.

"*My* donor has a flawless track record for making preggs that deliver within twenty-four hours of their due dates . . ."

If Ventura doesn't stop bragging about how her RePro scored in the highest percentile in every category measured by the Standards for Premium Ejaculated Reproductive Material, I will tie my tubes.

" . . . so I assume that Perfect will be no different."

Same goes for referring to her pregg as "Perfect."

Ventura picks up on my annoyance and runs with it as fast as a girl in her second trimester can run.

"All this bump talk must be soooooo boooooring for you, Melody. . . ."

"Um, no," I lie. "It's fascinating. Braxton-Hicks and epidurals and Kegels and . . . stuff."

I know I should be fascinated. But I'm not. And my trip to Babiez R U to try on FunBumps certainly didn't help in this regard.

"I'm sure you do," Ventura says crisply as the group around her giggles. And before I can make an effort to sound more convincing, she adds, "Oh, by the way, we passed Zen on his bicycle. . . ."

Ventura is obsessed with my friendship with Zen. She never fails to bring him up in conversation. "He's so hot! I don't know why you two don't just bump and get it over with," she says. "You'd really make such a cute pregg."

Everyone knows why Zen hasn't bumped me or anyone else: He's a risky investment. It doesn't matter that mixmatchy rainbow families are so on trend right now. High IQ can't make up for his insufficient verticality. Apparently that hasn't stopped him from giving gooooood everythingbut.

I stay calm. "I'm already under contract. You know that."

"I bet he'll be amped when you finally do pregg," Ventura says, casting a look around at the crowd. "Then you and Zen can bump-hump all you want without worrying about breaking your contract. . . ."

On any other day, I could just let this go. But today isn't an ordinary day, what with Harmony in hiding at my house and my parents trying to pimp me out and everything. I swear, if it weren't a felony, I'd smack Ventura AND her adorable six-month bump.

Fortunately, if unintentionally, Shoko comes to my rescue.

"Hey, there's nothing wrong with humping when you're bumping. Raimundo and I went at it like crazy for the full forty-two and my first pregg didn't come out all cock-knocked in the head."

Doing it for *fun*. The one advantage to bumping as an amateur.

"Omigod, I was just *scamming*!" Ventura lies. "See you at the meeting!" Then she shoots me a departing smirk and leads the pregnancy parade into the school.

"Waddle with me," Shoko says, taking my arm to hold me back. With an extra thirty pounds on her barely five-foot frame, she's on pace with one of those giant prehistoric ground sloths. The journey from the parking lot to her locker is epic, like moving from one era of geologic time into the next.

I'm still seething. "She acts as if she's the first girl in this school to go pro."

"She's scored a sweet deal," Shoko says, adjusting her belly band. "Full college tuition, tummy tuck, a car . . . "

"A car! She doesn't even have a license! And what's the big humping deal anyway? I've got all that written into *my* contract!"

Shoko levels me with a look that is barely more sympathetic than pathetic.

"Well, yes," she says, patting my shoulder. "But you haven't . . ."

Her eyes drop to my flat tummy.

"It's not my fault!" I cry.

"I know it's not."

We inch our way up the steps before I say what I really want to say.

"You think Ventura is the future of the Pro/Am, don't you?"

Shoko sighs with every ounce of extra poundage. "It's not that I think she *should* be."

"But you think she *is*."

Shoko's four chins nod.

"Oh, this is just breedy," I mutter. "Not even my best friend thinks I'm qualified to take over."

I don't mention how I know Malia would feel about it: *Break your contract while you still can!*

"There is a question of your commitment," Shoko says.

"My *commitment*?"

No one shows more commitment to school activities than I do! I'm president of the ECOmmunity Club, cocaptain of the soccer team (though we had to forfeit half of our season because we'd already lost Shoko and Malia when our striker was diagnosed with gestational diabetes), coach for the Science Olympiad . . .

Shoko grimaces, rubs her lower back. "Commitment to the *cause*," she explains. "To bringing together amateurs and professionals in the promotion of positive pregging."

"*I* was the first girl to sign a contract at this school! *I* made it the cool thing to do! And *I'm* not committed to the cause?"

"Well, not to be painfully obvious or anything, but it's not like you can, like, *authentically* represent the Alliance when you're the only unbump—"

"*Pre*bump!"

"Prebump. Whatever. But you *did* just turn sixteen," Shoko says with a sympathetic shake of her head. "You don't have much time left. . . ."

For the second time today, I'm brutally reminded of the repercussions of my looming obsolescence.

This is all Lib's fault. As my RePro Rep, Lib needs

to man up and start earning his 15 percent. It's his job to put more pressure on the Jaydens to hurry up and hire the Sperm to my Egg because my biological clock is ticking away.

I must look pretty depressed because Shoko abruptly changes the subject. "Gossip!"

My breath catches in my throat. I blinded the MiNet last night because I was studying—as always—but also because I felt like being antisocial. I don't care if there are MiFotos of Melody Mayflower standing next to a veiled and anonymous Church girl at the Mallplex. I could easily claim that she came faithing hard at me as Churchies are known to do. But if the MiNet is surging with MiFotos of Melody Mayflower standing next to an unveiled Church girl who looks *exactly like her,* I wanted to avoid those pics as long as possible. Would anyone believe I was being foto-bombed?

"Did you hear the latest about Malia?"

I can't exhale yet.

If I take credit for making it cool for Shoko, Ventura, and everyone else to pregg for profit, am I also to blame for what happened to Malia?

harmony
melody

THE DOORBELL RINGS.

I take a quick glance in the mirror, relieved to see more of Melody than myself. I inhale deeply, unlock and open the door.

It's Him. I mean, him.

"Yes, it's really me," he says, removing his mirrored sunglasses and flashing a smile.

Haloed in a golden light of the late-afternoon sun, Jondoe is more glorious in person than he was on-screen. Or in my dreams.

"There's no spontaneity in these transactions, nothing left to chance," he says, with a wide, bright grin. "Lib said you'd be here, so I thought I'd just connect in your facespace instead of the MiNet. I know you don't like the traditional trappings of romance like flowers, which you are *so right* in saying is ironic because you're Miss Melody May*flower* and all. . . ."

I almost correct him. Then I remember. *I am Miss Melody Mayflower.*

"So I brought your favorite brand of GlycoGoGo Bars and a sixer of Coke '99 instead."

He presents me with a clutch of soda cans in one hand and a box in the other. Then he gives me a knowing look and says, "We might need these later, you know, to keep our energy up," and laughs in a way that is meant to encourage me to laugh along with him. But I can't laugh, I can't accept his gifts, I can't do anything.

"I'm Jondoe," he purrs. "But you know that."

He bypasses the handshake and extends his arms wide, waiting for me to give him a welcoming embrace that I am in no condition to give. When I don't respond, he makes a clowny frowny face.

"Oh, come on, I'm not *that* bad, am I?" He's smiling again, teasing me.

He must know that he is the very opposite of bad. He is the finest evidence of goodness on this earth that I have ever encountered.

"You're disappointed. You think I'm hotter in the ads," he groans. But the smile is still there, fully confident that he could be no such thing to me or anyone. He speaks with cozy familiarity, as if we have known each other forever. "Oh, there's not enough Tocin in the world to get you to bump with me. . . ."

"Oh my grace!" I gasp at this sudden reminder of Jon-doe's intentions.

His face softens for a split second as it registers genu-ine surprise. "Ha ha ha!" He laughs beautifully, musically. "That's funny."

"I mean, um . . ."

My head fills with scrambled poetry from the Song of Songs, a book from the Old Testament that I've never cared much for before.

His mouth is sweetness itself; he is altogether lovely . . .

I cannot say such things! I will not! I swallow to clear my throat and try to speak.

"You look just like . . ."

Jesus.

He looks just like the Jesus in my dreams.

melody
harmony

I'M NOT PROUD TO SAY THAT I BLINDED MALIA AFTER HER LAST
MiNet rant.

They told me if I loved myself, if I loved my country I would
give Angelina to her rightful parents and never think about her
again. Why did you let them say those things to me? Why didn't
you try to stop them? You were my birthcoach. You were supposed
to be there for me. . . .

I just couldn't take the guilt anymore. I should have
known that wouldn't be the last I'd hear about her.

"Did she get out of the, um . . . you know, lockdown?"

"Over the weekend," Shoko says, leaning on my arm
for support. "Her parents are sending her to . . ." She looks
over her shoulders and whispers, "The Shields Center."

My intestines lurch. Only the worst cases get sent there,

mostly girls who go mad after misdelivering.

"She's totally lost it. Wackadoodledeedoo." Shoko crosses her eyes. "She was still wanking out and screaming to anyone who would listen that she's a victim of preggsploitation and that the deal was off and she was keeping her delivery for herself. She was even using the B word."

Where is my baby?

"Her parents are suing the RePro Rep for botching the whole transaction."

I don't blame them. Even before this postdelivery meltdown, we all talked about how Malia's broker was the worst. He totally lowballed her. True, she wasn't an easy sell. Malia is the nicest person I know, but niceness is not a quantifiable high-revenue quality. She's short and sorta thick in both meanings of the word—she struggled to keep up in her classes. But she was tough on the soccer field, a true team player who would sooner make an assist than go for the goal herself. So nice. Always so nice. I think she ran unopposed for vice president because we all felt like someone so nice deserved to excel at something. At least that's why *I* didn't run against her. (Ventura hadn't joined the Alliance yet. If she had, I doubt she would've had any such reservations because she's just that powertrippy.)

Malia was willing to deliver a pregg for someone who wanted one, either because she was really that nice or because the pressure to keep up with the rest of us— pressure that began the moment I signed my contract with Lib—was just too much. Or both. She didn't want to feel left out. And as the last prebump in the Alliance, I can hardly blame her.

Malia never disclosed the full terms of her contract but Shoko and I both have reason to believe that her Rep settled for something in the low four figures. When I told Lib about it, he told me it's quantity-over-quality brokers like that who give commercial surrogetting a bad name.

"It was *his* mistake for showing Malia the SimFant."

Surrogettes are never supposed to see 4-D because they supposedly come out really, really cute and we might get too attached. That's exactly what happened to Malia.

"You know they upped her dose of AntiTocin, right?"

"Right. And it wasn't enough?"

"Well, it *was* at first," Shoko says. "But it turns out that she stopped taking it for the last few months of pregging."

As I said, too much AntiTocin makes you a raving bitch for forty weeks straight. Too little and . . .

I want my baby.

"Malia can't remember to bring her flexbook to school every day; I should have known she'd forget to take her pill."

"Oh, she didn't forget," Shoko says brightly. "She confessed to her OB that she stopped taking her meds on purpose."

On purpose? I'm about to pop an outtie. "Why would she *ever* do that?"

"That's the best part." Shoko lights up. "She said it was making her fat!"

Shoko is laughing so hard that I'm surprised her delivery doesn't drop right here and now.

"It's not funny," I say.

"It is."

"It's not."

"She was pregging. She's *supposed* to get fat. How is that not funny?"

They took my baby.

"SHE'S OUR FRIEND AND SHE HAS POST-PARTUM PSYCHOSIS. HOW IS THAT FUNNY?"

"Oy." Shoko blanches, clutching her belly. "Keep your voice down. Burrito just kicked me in the kidneys."

"Sorry," I say without a trace of apology in my voice.

"It's just so Malia," Shoko says derisively. "Who else would stop taking AntiTocin on purpose?"

I could have prevented this. I should have done something as soon as she stopped calling her pregg Shrimpy and renamed it Angelina. I should have spoken up in the delivery room. I should have warned the doctors.

"I don't know how you can be so judgy about what's happened to her," I say, more to Shoko's stomach than to her. "You were pregg partners!"

For months I watched Shoko and Malia grow bigger by the day. I watched them swap MyTurnTees, share tubes of You Glow Girl! stretch-mark remover, and share bag after bag of Big Belly Jellies. I watched them bond with each other because they were forbidden to bond with their bumps. I watched them and thought I wanted to pregg right along with them.

Now I'm less excited to pregg than I am scared to be the only girl who hasn't.

"Oh please, I don't feel sorry for her at all," Shoko snaps, hands still rubbing her sides. "And if you had bumped already, you wouldn't either."

"What's *that* supposed to mean?"

"I know what it's like to look and feel like I've smuggled a watermelon up through my breedy bits, to need a half hour to waddle from the parking lot to my locker." She sighs heavily. "None of it is much fun, but pregging for the highest bidder was the best decision I could have ever made. If I had been traumatized by the experience, would I have agreed to do it again?"

I guessed that she would not.

"Reneggers like Malia make the rest of us look bad. If it keeps happening, it will be harder for Surrogettes to push for profit. Until you've walked a mile in my swollen feet, I doubt you'll be able to understand."

That's exactly why Malia picked me to be her birth-coach. As the only one who hadn't pregged yet, I was the only one who might listen to her pleas. She knew well before she was wheeled into the delivery room what she wanted to do. And if she had only trusted me enough to let me in on her secret, I might have tried to help her.

At least I'd like to think I would have.

By the time we reach Shoko's locker, I feel like I've walked a *million* miles in her swollen feet. This has been the longest, slowest trudge of my entire life.

"I'll see you at the meeting," I say.

"Uh-huh." She doesn't look at me.

I'm feeling for seriously sad as I press my way through the noisy, packed hallway to my own locker. The crowd doesn't part when they see *me* coming. . . .

Shoko and I never battled like this before she pregged. I've been blaming it on a combination of all-natural hormonal fluctuations plus synthetic ones brought on by AntiTocin. But maybe the tension between us has nothing to do with what's happening to her and everything to what's *not* happening to me.

A hand touches my shoulder from behind. Before I look, I know who it is.

"I'm sorry," Zen says.

I go for the hug, rest my chin on his shoulder, and hold on longer than necessary.

harmony

melody

I CAN'T SPEAK.

"So you were about to tell me how I look just like Jondoe from the Tocin ads," he says in a playful way. "I get that all the time."

I can't move.

He leans into the doorway trying to get a peek at the interior. "Are you going to let me in?"

"Oh my grace!" I jump to the side.

"Ha ha ha!" He laughs again. "That's funny. *You're* funny." He raises an eyebrow, as if we're sharing a secret. "The file didn't mention that you had a sense of humor."

He brushes past me and I breathe in his earthy-sweet scent.

"Whoa," he says, pausing at the two towers in the

common room. "This is an impressive collection of dead media."

He slips a square plastic case from the top of the stack and shows it to me. On it is a picture of a girl who looks to be around my own age, dressed in a tight red top and blasphemously short skirt. She's on her knees, but she's definitely not praying.

"You know the rappers Fed Double X?" Jondoe asks, without waiting for an answer. "This is their mom," he says, tapping the case. "She was a major bonermaker back in her prime." He glances up and gives me an appraising look. "You're way more reproaesthetical than she ever was." Jondoe carefully puts the case back where it came from.

I bite my lip to stop myself from yelping, but a squeal comes out just the same. He turns away from the rack and gives me a quizzical look, as though he's not certain whether the sound came from me or a small rodent.

"So. Your story," he says.

I wring my gloveless hands. "My story?"

"Yeah, your story," he says, stretching his arms above his head to touch the fleur-de-lis pattern in the pressed tin ceiling. "Why you decided to become a Surrogette . . ." His slim white T inches up, revealing too much.

"Oh my grace," I exclaim, again without thinking. I cover my mouth with my hands.

"Oh *my* grace!" he repeats for the second time, covering his mouth with his hands. Then he laughs the deep-in-the-belly laugh. "Ha ha ha ha ha! Your file didn't say you'd be funny," he says again. "And you, Miss Melody Mayflower, are funny."

I am Miss Melody Mayflower.

"You're a trailblazer," Jondoe says, running a hand along the irregular tree scraps jutting out of the walls. "I'm impressed. The first girl at your school to popularize reproductive empowerment."

"Right," I say, numbly nodding.

"All that, and smart too! So you're applying to Global U. I guess you're ready to expand your horizons?"

"Expand my horizons," I say truthfully. "Definitely."

We stop in front of a half-open door. He cranes his neck to take a peek.

"And this is your bedroom."

melody
harmony

NOT MUCH IN THE WAY OF VALUABLE EDUCATION HAPPENED
today. If my parents had any idea, they would've made up
for the wasted day by scheduling an after-school session with
one of my academic drill instructors. Their cluelessness is by
far the best thing about the schoolwide MiNet blind.

In first period, Luciana Holquist, Eiko Cooper, Dea Lan,
and Brynn Mandelbaum interrupted the Mandarin lesson by
requesting passes to the nurse's office. They're the Cheerclones
who tried to synchro-bump with the select members of the
varsity basketball team known as the Ballers at the masSEX
party Zen chauffeured the other night. They just couldn't
wait until the end of the day to see if they had succeeded.
So it was all anyone could talk about for the rest of the class
period because the biggest synchro-bump at our school so far

happened last fall when three girls I coached on the Science Olympiad were tri-sperminated by Maxim, the only Olympian over five ten whose whole body wasn't armored by acne. This was a challenging conversation to have in Mandarin, however, because we haven't learned the words for "Cheerclones," "Ballers," "sperminated," or "masSEX parties."

It turned out that the Cheerclones were far less successful than the Science Olympians, who had the left-sided brainskills necessary for accurately calculating ovulation. When only Dea returned with a plus sign, the rest of first period and all of second period calculus was spent congratulating her and consoling the rest of the squad.

"You can always try again tomorrow!" Zen said encouragingly to Luciana, Eiko, and Brynn. "Why wait until tomorrow? How about right now? I've got five minutes!" He was determined to put the cheer back in Cheerclone. "Oh, I get it. You're in a rush! I'll do it in two!"

"Oh, Zen!" They giggled through their tears.

And then one of them—maybe Eiko, who can tell?—said something weird.

"You totally owe us for bailing the other night."

But before I could find out what she was talking about, the bell rang and Zen bolted out of the classroom for his favorite class, an elective on the Decline of Western Civilization.

My third period is Personal Health and Fitness. The girls in my class who were legitimately bent over with nausea in the bleachers were joined by so many others who were green with Sympathetic Morning Sickness that I had no choice but to join the boys in their soccer game, which was fine because after thousands of hours of drills and skills, I'm faster and have better footwork than half of them already and the other half had total-body hangovers from the weekend and could barely touch their toes to the ball without flinching in pain.

Periods four (North American Language Arts and Culture) and five (Biogenetics II) were spent reading and responding to all the notes Zen was passing me now that he had brought comic relief to the Cheerclones and was back to obsessing about my sister. Since our school went MiNet blind, it's for seriously more like 1836 than 2036.

I THINK YOUR SISTER'S MARRIAGE IS A MISTAKE.

I think you're a victim of your own false consciousness.

YOU HAVE MANY UPMARKET QUALITIES BUT A SENSE OF HUMOR IS NOT ONE OF THEM. FOR SERIOUS, THOUGH. DON'T YOU THINK IT'S STRANGE THAT SHE NEVER TALKS ABOUT HER FIANCÉ? OR HER WEDDING PLANS? WHEN MY SISTER WAS ENGAGED HER WEDDING WAS ALL SHE TALKED ABOUT. AND SHE WASN'T EVEN A VIRGIN. HARMONY HAS A LOT MORE TO LOOK FORWARD TO ON HER HONEYMOON. . . .

The Jaydens aren't paying me for my sense of humor. What are you being paid for? And I did notice. But most of what they do in Goodside is strange. Why should this be any different?

NO PRICE TAG CAN BE PUT ON MY SKILL SET. BUT DON'T GET
ME OFF TOPIC. WE SHOULD OFFER YOUR SISTER ASYLUM SO SHE CAN
STAY IN OTHERSIDE. FORCING MARRIAGE IS A VIOLATION OF HER
BASIC HUMAN RIGHTS.

What makes you think she wants to stay here?

I'VE DONE MY RESEARCH. MOST TRUBIES DON'T GET FIVE MILES
AWAY FROM THEIR SETTLEMENT BEFORE THEY GET SCARED, GO
BACK, AND MAKE A LIFELONG COMMITMENT TO THE CHURCH. THAT
SHE CAME HERE AT ALL PROVES THAT SHE WANTS TO STAY.

What if I don't want her to stay here?

IF YOU CHOOSE TO BE SO UNCOOL AND CAST OUT YOUR IDENTICAL
TWIN SISTER, THEN SHE CAN ALWAYS STAY WITH ME.

Won't the Cheerclones get jealous? And how exactly
did you bail on them Saturday night?

YOUR SISTER IS TOO IMPORTANT TO WASTE TIME GOSSIPING
ABOUT HOW I SPENT SATURDAY NIGHT. THIS IS A SERIOUS SITUATION,
MEL. YOU HAVE AN OPPORTUNITY TO DO SOMETHING HERE. TO
HELP.
THIS TIME DON'T WAIT UNTIL IT'S TOO LATE.

Wise enough not to mention Malia by name, Zen
made the most winning argument he possibly could.

harmony
melody

JONDOE PUSHES OPEN THE DOOR, SWEEPS INSIDE THE bedroom, then heads straight to the floor-to-ceiling windows. He taps the blinds so they raise up to reveal a view of the woodsy backyard. A creamy sunbeam fills the room. Without warning, he strips off his long-sleeved white shirt, under which he's wearing an even more formfitting sleeveless shirt. Across his chest spreads lettering I'm afraid to look at.

Despite my better instincts, I read them anyway:

OPEN UP WITH TOCIN.

I feel dizzy and my tongue tastes like rust.

"Come here," he says, still looking out the window. "What do you see out there?"

"Trees," I croak.

"Right," he replies with a wry smile. "Trees."

Then he turns, puts his arms around me, and pulls me toward the glass.

His left arm is under my head, and his right arm embraces me. . . .

"Smile, Miss Melody Mayflower," he whispers in my ear.

Then just as quickly he abandons me to examine the wall covered in Melody's MiFoto collage.

"This is your best friend, Zen," he says, picking him out from a group photo taken at the Science Olympiad. His face gets grim. "Insufficient verticality must be a major bonerkiller."

He points to a woman with her legs scissoring in mid-air, a ball floating on the flat of her shoelaces. "Ah yes, number fifteen, your favorite player on the U.S. national team."

He drags a soccer ball out of corner with his foot. "I play too. But you know that." He flips the ball in and out and up and around and over and through his two feet. It's all a blur.

"Ready? Your turn," he says, before passing the ball to me. But I'm not ready at all and it hits me in the knees and bounces back to the floor with a dull thud. Athleticism, apparently, is not something I share with my sister.

"Sorry," he says flatly. "I figured . . ." He stops midthought, starts again, lights up with another smile. He spots a guitar case in the corner. "I think it's cool that you play real guitar instead of guitarbot."

Melody plays guitar? I had no idea she had an interest in music! So do I! We have more in common than I thought.

"Play something for me."

"I don't know . . ." I say. I'm in the worship band back at home, but I don't know how to play any songs that are popular in Otherside.

"I've seen your file, I know you're talented. I'd like to hear you live."

Then he gets down on his knees in front of me and presses his hands together in prayer.

"Pleeeeeeeease?"

I nod yes, if only to get him up off the floor. A few more seconds and there would be nothing, and I mean nothing, I could do to stop myself from getting down on the floor with him. . . .

To pray!

He claps his hands, hops to his feet, and jumps back onto Melody's bed. He contentedly rolls among her pillows and blankets as if it's the most natural thing in the world.

I take the guitar and pluck some notes to see if it's in tune.

"Go on," he says, gazing up at me from his supine position.

Then, with my eyes closed, I sing a simple hymn to give me strength:

*"Love on me
Love in me
Love through me
Jesus."*

I sing it like I've never sung it before.

*"Love on you
Love in you
Love through you
Jesus."*

And as I do, I feel a tiny flame sparking deep inside me, the flicker of a single lit match in a place I'm not supposed to think about, and as I keep singing and strumming that light burns hotter and brighter and spreads its warmth up and out and throughout my entire body, and I sing and sing and sing until that tiny torch has set my entire body ablaze, an undousable conflagration of passion.

melody
harmony

WITH SO MUCH GOING ON TODAY I COULD BARELY FOCUS ON my flexbooks. The upside is that I've been too distracted to worry about what will happen once I catch up with Shoko for the Pro/Am meeting. I see her before she sees me, which isn't surprising because she's as wide as she is tall.

"Hey," I say.

"Hey," she says back. "I passed my mucus plug today! You know what that means! Burrito won't be far behind!"

Gaaaah. Why am I the only one who gets icked by talk like this? I've got to pull myself together.

"That's breedy! Get ready for payday!"

"Yeah," she says, rubbing the small of her back. "I'm just surprised. I thought Burrito would squat for a full forty-two weeks. . . ."

I catch Ventura and her adorable six-month bump making her way toward the classroom where the meeting is about take place.

"I'm sorry about this morning." This time I mean it.

"It's okay," says Shoko. "I've been thinking about it and, you know, I'd be wanky too if Malia was MiNetting me all the time about keeping my legs closed and not making the same mistake she did."

Malia isn't flaming me. She's warning me. Or trying to. Before it's too late . . .

"She's obviously not in her right mind right now. Hopefully she'll get whatever therapy she needs at the Shields Center, and by the time she gets back you'll already have delivered a pregg to prove that she was all wrong."

Ventura is almost within earshot. I don't want her making smirky contributions to this conversation. Thankfully, the conversation ends midsentence in a familiar way.

"Oy! I gotta pee."

"Wait," I say as she turns, "before you go!"

She smiles as I place both hands on her belly and rub it for luck.

harmony
melody

WHEN I OPEN MY EYES, I SEE JONDOE GAPING AT ME IN UTTER wonder.

"That was . . ." He opens and closes his mouth a few times. For the first time since I met him at the door, he's at a loss for words. Our eyes are locked for a few seconds of silence, and I'm thinking that I could live the rest of my life like this, just gazing into his limitless eyes, when he breaks the connection with a word.

"Unexpected."

Jondoe pulls his knapsack onto his lap, reaches in and pulls out a thin white stick wrapped in plastic. He points it at me. I must look as thoroughly confused as I feel.

"You don't know what this is," he says, more of a comment than a question.

I shake my head.

"Whoa," he says with honest wonderment. "You're like a nubie. Innocent," he says in a quieter voice as he unwraps the plastic. "Surprising."

He opens his mouth, and gestures for me to do the same. I open my mouth and he laughs again.

"I can't do it from all the way over here!"

He beckons me to come away from the window and without hesitation I float over to him without my feet touching the ground. We are too close now. I'm feeling hot and swoony again, like I did in the Mallplex yesterday, as if I'm being smothered by a veil made of soaking-wet wool.

"Ahh," he says, presenting his open mouth to me with his tongue out.

"Ahh . . ."

Let him kiss me with the kisses of his mouth: for your love is more delightful than wine. . . .

He tenderly inserts the stick under my tongue, then pulls away and flops back onto the bed.

"Close and hold for ten seconds."

I do as he says, which isn't easy because my chin and the rest of my body are trembling. I realize now that the stick is a kind of thermometer. I watch as the white plastic turns bright green.

He swings into a sitting position on the edge of the bed, feet firmly planted on the floor. He pats the mattress, inviting me to sit down beside him. I shake my head, no.

135

I'm fine just where I am on the other side of the room, my back up against the wall.

He comes to me.

"Well," he says, pulling out the stick from between my lips, "it's a good thing I came today."

"It is?"

"Green means go!"

Green means go. I think of my green fertility gown hanging in my closet back in Goodside. Never worn.

"You're peaking." He tosses the stick into the recycling bin. "We can bump this out tonight."

Jondoe claps his hands and rubs them together, like he's warming himself up in front of a fire.

I gulp loud enough for God Himself to hear.

melody
harmony

VENTURA VIDA HAS THE PEE STICK.

"The Pro/Am has an image problem," she says. "We're just not *sexy* enough. I mean, rilly!"

We reviewed the fund-and-awareness-raising success of "Why Save Yourself When You Can Save the World?" T-shirt sale. We signed a petition to get caf services to offer more fertile, high-folate versions of pizza and french fries because we're gagging on the spinach and chickpeas in the salad bar. It's the last meeting of the year, so there's nothing else on the Pro/Am agenda except the vote for the next president. But this won't happen until Ventura surrenders the pee stick. And she's clutching the gold-plated positive pregnancy test like a talisman, unwilling to let it go and let someone else get a word in edgewise.

"Princeton Day Academy is already on track to rack up forty-two preggs this year. That's double last year's tally, but accounts for only twenty-five percent of our school's fertile female population! We shouldn't be satisfied until every Little Tiger is wearing one of these!"

She grasps the necklace that we all wear. Earlier in the meeting Ventura proudly added another bead to her chain during the Gestation Celebration, when all girls earn a bronze, silver, or gold bead for entering their first, second, and third trimesters, respectively. Everyone gets a glass bead just for joining, and births are commemorated with a diamond or rhinestone. Professionals usually have enough cash extra for the former, while amateurs have to settle for the latter—a good example of the type of thing that causes tension and called for the creation of the Alliance in the first place.

As if reading my mind, Ventura says, "We've gone so far in putting our petty differences as professionals and amateurs aside. We can come together as a united front to make girls do the right thing and bump like all of us." She makes a big show out of turning her head to look at me. "I mean, *almost all* of us."

Drawing attention to the embarrassingly blingless chain around my neck is totally uncalled for, even for Ventura.

"We owe it to our community, both locally and globally, to try even harder to do better."

"Maybe we should follow China's lead with mandatory

inseminations," I mutter to Shoko, hoping to get her attention.

Shoko's sitting right next to me, but she's too busy digging through a bag of Big Belly Jellies to acknowledge what I've said. Apparently Ventura did hear me because she holds up the pee stick and makes a slashing gesture across her throat. Gah, she has nerve for a new girl. I make a big show out of putting my hand in the air, a gesture that she just as elaborately ignores.

"The new man brands are getting way too much attention. You've all seen the Tocin ads. . . ."

The room explodes with everyone's favorite studs-for-hire.

"For serious. How hot is Phoenix?"

"I want me some Fitch!"

"Jondoe! Omigod! Jondoe!"

"Yes, they're all major stiffies," Ventura yells over the chatter. "But it shouldn't be about them! It should be about us!" She pops her belly out in a provocative bump-and-grind. "Can't PREGG without the . . ."

"EGG!" shout Tulie Peters (sophomore, amateur, eighteen weeks) and Dyanna Merrill (senior, professional, fourteen weeks) in unison. They obviously practiced this call-and-response before the meeting. I have to give Ventura credit for getting a professional and an amateur to chant together in the spirit of bipartisan pregging. I'd also like to point out that you also can't PREGG without the SPERM, but highlighting such contradictions in Ventura's logic would go over like a raging case of hemorrhoids.

Shoko's hazy expression suddenly snaps into focus as she holds a creamy yellow Big Belly Jelly between her swollen fingers.

"Lemon ginger!" she says to no one in particular. "Aids the digestion." She pops it into her mouth and then, as an aside, in between chews: "Burrito's got his foot stuck in my poop chute."

I snort with laughter.

"Excuse me," Ventura says sharply. "I'm the one with the pee stick. *I've* still got the floor."

"Sorry, Ventura," Shoko says. "Burrito is making me stooooopid. I can't stay focused for . . . um . . . you know . . . *shit.*"

Heads all around the circle nod in sympathy.

"Well, that's all the more reason to vote before you go on birthleave," says Ventura, tossing her glossy black hair over her shoulder. Ventura for seriously lucked out on the hormonal draw because her hair is more lustrous now than ever before. Poor Celine Lichtblau (freshman, amateur, eleven weeks) is losing her hair by the handful and she's still got two trimesters left. By the time she reaches her due date, she'll be balder than the delivery she pushes out in the stirrups.

I'm now shaking my hand like a Cheerclone without her pom-poms. Shoko's face is back in the Big Belly Jellies. Ventura and her adorable six-month bump stand up and look over and beyond our little group, assuming a self-important posture as if she's about to address a crowd of thousands, not tens.

"If I'm so lucky to be voted our next president today," Ventura says, winking at the group, "I'll make it my mission to rilly overhaul our image. We need to get sexier to attract more girls to our cause."

She puts on her most life-or-death serious face.

"I know you're all aware of the unfortunate circumstances that led to the dismissal of our former vice president."

The whole room titters nervously. Ventura's tone is somber, and yet her heart-shaped face takes on an even rosier glow.

"We live in frightening times, girls, and we need to be role models, not reneggers."

Oh, no. I can already see where she's going with this.

"It's our duty to work together as professionals and amateurs to promote positive pregging for the sake of all the parental units who desperately want our deliveries. Do you appreciate how lucky we are to live in a true melting pot of races, ethnicities, and cultures? In the United States, deliveries of every color and creed are *valued*. Do you know that if we lived in the Middle East, or parts of Europe, we would be forced by law to pregg with our own kind to keep the gene pool pure?" A ripple of gasps moves through the group. "I know. It's shocking to think that the government would try to stick its nose in our ladyparts."

I'm hoping Shoko will break in with a joke about

Burrito sticking his nose in her ladyparts, but she's as hypnotized as the rest of them.

"Our mixmatchy preggs are the best way to promote peace around the world. Who are you going to hate if you have blood running through you from every continent?" She casts a sly glance in my direction. "That is, unless you're like Melody here, who's so pure that no swimmers are worthy of her womb. . . . *Just scamming!*"

Barely muffled laughter all around the room.

I hate Ventura Vida. I want to draw blood. And I'm *not* scamming.

"For the first time in history, teenage girls are *the most important people on the planet.*" She sings the last few words, of course. "We can't all be like Zorah Harding, who, as we all know, is due to make her ninth and tenth deliveries any moment now!"

The room breaks into applause for the most famously prolific eighteen-year-old in America.

"But we can all aspire to her greatness, can't we? Whether you're an amateur"—and she pauses to look meaningfully at Celine and Tulie—"or a professional Surrogette"—she stops again to lock eyes with Dyanna and a captivated Shoko—"our nation needs *all* our preggs, girls, if we have any chance of reclaiming our undisputed status as the most powerful country in the world well into the twenty-first century and beyond. If we hesitate"—and now she slowly turns her head in my direction again—"our multicultural American society, a shining beacon of tolerance and empathy around the world, will die. I mean, like, rilly *rilly* die."

Everyone is on their swollen feet. Everyone, including my best friend. Some are clapping, some are crying, all are rocking their huge bellies with patriotic pride. I imagine an army of unseen deliveries pumping tiny fists. "USA! USA! USA!"

Even before the votes are cast—all but two (thanks, Shoko) in Ventura's favor—there's no doubt in my mind that I am rilly, *rilly* humped.

harmony
melody

"TONIGHT?"

A look of disappointment crosses Jondoe face. "I know," he says apologetically. "I also wish we could get down to business right now," he says with a wolfish smile. "But you're my fourth call of the day. Even *I* need down-time to reload."

The fire deep in my belly shows no sign of fizzling out.

"On the upside, we've got a few hours to make some media."

He suddenly jumps up, heads to the windows, looks outside. He flexes his arms above his head, flashes a smile, holds completely still for a few beats, then drops his arms and the smile.

"What?" How is it possible to be so enthralled by

someone I can barely understand?

"You didn't get the itinerary?" His face contorts in something resembling anger for the first time. "My assistant should have messaged you earlier. This is totally unprofessional!" He sighs heavily. "We're going to all your favorite places. The Avatarcade, then the All-Sports Arena, followed by dinner at the U.S. Buff-A . . ."

This all sounds very exciting. "So it's a *date*?"

"A date? I've never been on a *date*."

"Me either," I say truthfully. We don't date in Goodside. We marry.

"I've had good hangs, but a date?" He can't stop smiling at me. "I don't think I've ever heard anyone under a hundred years old use that word. Though it *is* kind of cute . . ."

He starts walking out of the room before looking back behind him.

"Are you coming with me or not?"

Come, my darling, my beautiful one, come with me . . .

I nod yes before I can say no.

melody
harmony

I'M IGNORING MORE THAN 250 MESSAGES MINETTED WHILE I AM in school. I can wait until I get home to check them. I'm in no rush for 250 variations on SORRY U LOST.

The MiNet blind actually extends a hundred yards in all directions around our campus. About a dozen students are clustered on the first unblinded patch of sidewalk, too eager to catch up on eight technology-free hours to walk another step. The MiGamers are the most dangerous because they're too busy racing, blowing up, or otherwise challenging competitors in the virtual world to pay attention to people in the real world. Just last week a MiGamer was kickboxing a demonic gnome in Troll Troopers 4: Garden of Good and Evil and accidentally skulled a freshman mathlete with his foot. (The mathlete, of course, was too focused on his own chess match against a twelve-year-old Russian prodigy to get out of harm's way.) Those on MiTunes or MiChat don't jump around as much, but tend to sing or talk way out loud.

"It's human nay-cha . . ."

"And he was like, WHOO-HOO . . ."

"For me to sperminay-cha . . ."

"And I was like, NUH-UH."

"I wanna impregnay-cha . . ."

All of it contributes to the noisy muddle of nonsense that I can't get away from far or fast enough. One of the sidewalk MiChatters is Zen, wearing black shorts and a tiger-striped zip-front jacket. He must have had a match this afternoon.

"Dude, I'm telling you. If you're *serious* about the game, you've got to stop spreading your seed around. When I've got an important match, I store enough *hornergy* to power up every electricar on the eastern seaboard. . . ."

"Hornergy" is Zen's term for the indomitable athletic edge powered by sexual restraint. The basketball, baseball, and football teams haven't had a winning season in years. The table-tennis team, however, is undefeated.

I weave my bike in and out of the babbling crowd and don't even wait to see if he notices me. I'm about to pass right by him when he holds out his arm to stop me.

"Wait," he says. Then he unfocuses his attention and says, "Later, bro," to whomever he was MiChatting with, before winking, blinking, and shutting it off and fixing his attention back on me.

"I was just giving some advice to the captain of the lacrosse team," he says. "They lost again."

"Oh," I say.

"You lost too," he says, walking his bike alongside mine.

"Ventura sure didn't waste any time in alerting the MiNet, did she?"

Zen rakes his scalp. "I don't know why you even wanted to run in the first place," he says. "How does a virge on the verge represent the interests of the Pro/Am Alliance?"

I sigh. "Shoko said the same thing. Did you guys co-write your script? And don't call me that."

"What?"

"A virgin on the verge of obsolescence. It's offensive."

"Well, it's true, isn't it?"

I halt my bike. "It's *not* true. I have at least a year left to bump!" I hate having to defend myself to Zen of all people. "And unless you've got some cure for the Virus that you're keeping to yourself instead of sharing it with the world and going down in history as the hero who rescued humanity from its slow trudge toward mass extinction, then you're also on the clock. If I'm a virge on the verge, so are you."

"And so we are," he says in a satisfied voice. "Beep. Beep. Beep. *Boom*."

We climb onto our bikes and ride together in a tense

silence—him in front, me following behind. At a red light, Zen reaches out and—*RING! RING!*—triggers my bell. The he looks up at me with total seriousness.

"I know what would solve all our problems."

"What?"

"It's human nay-cha . . . For me to sperminay-cha. . . ."

I have to laugh. For serious, life would be so much easier if I could just take Zen up on his offer, make good on our secret pact, and get the whole thing over with already. Maybe it could even solve my parents' financial problems. I mean, if Shoko and Raimundo could make out so well in their postdelivery bidding . . .

Who am I kidding? No one who can pay serious money would be willing to take the risk on Zen.

Zen is humping his bicycle as he sings, *"Don't hesitaycha . . . Or it will be too lay-cha. . . ."*

I punch him in the arm, then move forward at the sight of the green light.

"Hey, watch it, there," Zen says. "This arm belongs to the number one table-tennis player in the county."

"I'm sorry," I say. "I forgot to even ask about your match. Did you win?"

"No need to ask. Of course I won," he says. "Mel, my hornergy could end our country's use of fossil fuels once and for all. I was just telling the lacrosse guys that I can thank my virge-on-the-verge-ness for my total dominance over all my opponents."

I clutch a hand to my chest, pretending to swoon.

"And to think you would have given it all up just to cheer me up."

I *am* feeling better. Losing to Ventura doesn't seem like the omnicidal tragedy it was a half hour ago. Such is the power of Zen.

"I wasn't just offering to help you," he says grandly. "But all of humanity."

"Oh, *really*?"

He pauses for effect. "I'm starting to agree with the ranters who think the world is overpopulated with all the wrong people."

I choke as if I've just swallowed a soccer ball. Just when I'm about to accuse Zen of being the unlikeliest eugenicist, he explains himself.

"*Old* people," he explains. "There are too many old people with their old ideas and not enough new people with new ideas. We are in a state of cultural stagnation— I mean, the last great technological innovation was the MiNet, and that's been around for more than a decade. Did you ever stop to think about why we drink Coke '99? Because old people want the formula they drank when when they were young like us."

"But I like Coke '99. . . ."

"Of course you love it! Because all the old people who control all of mass media and commercial enterprises have manipulated the system to bend to their grampy whims! Old people control everything because there are so many more of them than there ever will be of us. Unless we want to wait until our parents' generation finally takes a dirtnap, it's up to thinking people like you and me to come together and create the next generation of innovators and game-changers. . . ."

I stop my bike and look Zen straight in the eye.

"Do you really believe this? Or are you still trying to have sex with me?"

Zen grins. "A skilled debater always knows how to win both sides of an argument."

harmony
melody

I FOLLOW JONDOE OUT OF THE ROOM, DOWN THE HALL TOWARD the entrance to the house. He stops right before the front door, looks me up and down.

"Are you sure you want to wear your hair like that?"

I touch my braid.

"It's just that I always saw you with your hair down, except when you were on the soccer field."

Every girl in our settlement wears her hair in a single braid. It's one less distraction that can keep us focused on faith. I remove the elastic, and pull out the plaits, and let my hair loose. Something deeper and more fundamentally *me* is coming apart too. . . .

"Relax," Jondoe says. "Let the pro handle it. I'll do all the talking. Just remember to smile."

And before I get to ask him why, the mirrored sunglasses go on and his teeth come out. He opens the front door and I am blinded by intense beams of light shooting at me from all directions.

This is it! The end! The Rapture!

Lights flash all around us, and I falter on wobbly knees. Jondoe puts his arm around me protectively, pulls me to his car, opens the door, gently shoves me inside, and closes the door behind me. I want to tell him it's no use trying to get away in his car, the angels find us and carry us away no matter where or how well we hide. I'm screaming on the inside, I can't get any of the words out. He, however, is unshaken. Jondoe rushes around to the driver's side, opens the door, and slips in beside me.

Before he shuts the door he leans out and shouts, "Suck on this, scummers!"

Then he starts the engine, stomps the foot pedal, and we make our escape in a swirling dust bowl of gray earth and gravel.

melody
harmony

WE DON'T SAY ANYTHING UNTIL MY HOUSE IS IN SIGHT.

"So what's the plan?" Zen asks.

"What's *what* plan?"

"How are we going to get your sister to stay?"

"Not that again," I huff. "She's a person, not one of your causes."

"People *are* my cause."

Unlike Zen, I didn't think much about Harmony all day. After being alone in the house for hours, I imagine that Harmony is eager to see me. Did she *really* amuse herself all day by reading the Bible? I get to the front door and I notice that she's left it unlocked. I'll need to remind Harmony that even though we're not in a high-crime zone, we're not on the farm anymore either.

"Hey, Harmony," I call out. "I'm home."

No response.

Zen comes in behind me. "Where's my favorite Good-sider?"

No response. The silence makes me uneasy.

"Maybe she's taking a nap," I say unconvincingly. When I check the guest room I'm not surprised that it's empty.

"Maybe she went back home," Zen says, clearly disappointed.

"Her suitcase is still here." As is the dress she was wearing when I left this morning, which is folded neatly on her bed . . . next to her veil.

This isn't good.

Zen pulls on his hair. "I'll check to see if she left a note or something."

I head down the hall and peek inside my room, thinking she might have slept in there again, as she doesn't know I know she did last night. (I didn't say anything to her about it because I didn't want to make her feel more blinked than she very clearly already felt at breakfast this morning.) Though there are signs that she was definitely in here at some point during the day—my bedspread is messed up—she isn't there now.

"No note," Zen says.

I start to worry now. If I knew she was back in Good-side, I'd be fine. But all signs point to her being on the loose in Princeton, probably faithing hard in Palmer

Square, asking people I know if they have God . . .

"Zen! She went out without her veil! Everyone will think she's me!"

"So what?"

"What's to stop her from marching up to Ventura Vida and quoting—oh, I don't know—the book of Virgin Mary chapter whatever, which says, *'Thou art a dirty whore and thy pregg is a bastard and thou wilt burn in hell'*?"

Zen stops dead. "Does the Bible really say that?"

"YES!" I scream.

"Dose down," Zen says, his eyeballs flicking wildly in his sockets. "There's nothing new on the MiNet about you. Just the same stuff about getting humped by Ventura in the election. And if she does show up, you can always say it's a prank. . . ."

I scan the unread MiNet queue for the day, thinking maybe Harmony somehow tried to contact me while I was at school. There are few from my parents, a dozen nonsense messages from Lib asking random questions like RU TERMIN8ED? HOW IZZE? and tons of scamspam claiming to be Jondoe of all people telling me how repro-aesthetical I am and how special and surprising I am and how he's never met a girl like me before. Gah. Are there any girls out there who are gullible enough to believe that the hottest RePro in the world wants to MiChat them up?

I know I should be focusing on my missing twin, but I can't stop thinking about the number of messages from Lib. He's in Stockholm right now scouting for Scandinavian talent. I haven't heard from him in weeks and to get so many in such a short amount of time must mean *something* even if I can't make any sense of what that something might be right now. My curiosity is about to get the better of me when the doorbell rings.

"Harmony!" Zen and I shout simultaneously.

I race to the front door. As annoyed as I am that she's still *here*, I'm relieved that she's not *out there* providing Ventura Vida and the rest of the Pro/Am with a new excuse to kick me out of the club entirely.

I fling open the door, amped to unleash a version of my own parents' favorite lectures about personal responsibility, when I'm confronted not with Harmony at all, but a hulking teenage boy I've never seen before in my life.

"It's you," he says simply.

This fair-haired, ruddy-faced stranger is wearing a straight-cut black suit and a white shirt buttoned to his thick neck, no tie. A black, broad-brimmed felt hat sits on his head, and muddy lace-up work boots are on his feet. Behind him is a beat-up suitcase very similar to the one Harmony brought with her yesterday.

"One guess where's he's from," Zen says, reading my mind.

He makes a move to hug me with massively muscled arms.

"Back off, farmboy!" I snap back. "I don't know who *you* are! But I'm not who you think *I* am."

He looks bashfully at his feet. I've embarrassed him.

"You're twin sisters." Then he mumbles something else that sounds like "shoulda known."

"Yes, I'm Melody," I say. "And you must be Ram."

"Ma'am," he stammers, eyes back on this boots.

"Ma'am!" Zen thinks this is hilarious.

"You look just like her." Ram's lips barely move when he talks. It's a wonder I can make out any words at all.

"Well, we *are* identical twins," I say. "That's usually how it works."

He looks at the ground and says nothing. He wears his suit uncomfortably, as if it's two sizes two small. His shoulders are hunched up around his ears but his arms hang heavy at his sides, like he's carrying burlap sacks of flour or cornmeal or whatever he carries in burlap sacks around Goodside.

"Unfortunately, your fiancée isn't here," Zen says.

"My *what?*" Ram asks, a genial if befuddled smile on his face.

I don't understand what's going on here, and it's not only because I need a translation app to decode Ram's mush-mouthed mangling of the English language.

"Har-mo-ny," Zen says, speaking very slowly and deliberately. *"Mel-o-dy's twin sis-ter."*

"Right," Ram says, now looking anywhere but at us. "Your twin."

Then he raises his left arm and holds up his left hand, revealing a solid-gold band on his fourth finger. Having remained impossibly still throughout this conversation

158

up to now, this modest gesture has the attention-stealing impact of Jondoe's half-naked humpdancing in the infamous Tocin commercial. But that's nothing compared to what he says next.

"And my wife."

THIRD

We shouldn't be using hardworking American tax-
payer dollars to pay Americans to pregg because
pregging is patriotic and America is the greatest nation
under God, so God bless America and Americans!
—"Mission: Maternity," Fox and Freedom Party

melody
harmony

ZEN'S BOPPING HIS HIPS BACK AND FORTH, WAGGLING HIS finger in whole world's face, mimicking the famous moves that go along with Fed Double X's first hit, "Toldja (So)."

"I toldja toldja . . . Coulda bought and soldja soldja. . . ."

Zen is never happier than when finding out that one of his hypotheticals isn't so hypothetical after all.

"I toldja toldja toldja toldja soooooooo. . . ."

I grab a pillow and two-handed hurl it at Zen with all my might. It takes him out at the knees and he keels over.

"AAARGH. WATCH THE ARM. . . ."

Meanwhile Ram is lying on my couch with his eyes closed, wearing a cold-pack helmet that has saved my brain after countless soccer balls to the skull. Because Ram sure sounds like he suffered a major blow to the head, this helmet was my best attempt at trying to make him feel better.

"Harmony isn't here?" Ram asks for the dozenth time.

He clearly isn't the most communicative person on his best days, let alone after finding out that his wife has vanished off the grid.

"Where could she be?"

"We don't know. She didn't leave a message. Her suitcase is still here, though."

Zen speaks for both of us because I too have lost the ability to communicate intelligibly let alone intelligently.

"She can't go far," Ram says. "Her cabdriver told me she traded her ring to pay for her trip."

"Her wedding ring?" Zen asks.

Another nod.

"Oooh, that's cold."

I remember the edge in Harmony's voice when the Babiez R U salesgirl asked whether she was wearing a ring under her glove. No wonder she got so defensive!

"It wasn't worth much." Ram's voice sounds high and hysterical now, like it's being strangled in the back of this throat. "But it was the best I could do."

And then he presses his face into his hands to hide his tears.

I shoot Zen a panicked "Now what?" look. I'm really not good at stuff like this. Touchy-feely stuff. I mean, I aced the EQ exam, but that's only because my parents hired a tutor to drill me in all matters emotional.

Zen brings his arms together in a circle and panto-
mimes a way overdue pregg.

"What?" I mouth.

Zen now strokes his bodacious invisible bump.

"Why are you pretending to pregg?"

Ram opens his eyes to see this.

"I'm pretending to *hug*," Zens wails in exasperation.
"This man needs a hug."

When I don't go for it, he starts ripping his hair out.

"GIVE HIM A HUG."

Ram pushes his palm at me. "No, ma'am."

Zen chuckles again at "ma'am."

"That ain't right. I am a married man." This message is
as clear as it gets. Then his eyes well up again.

"Why don't YOU hug him, Zen?"

"Naw!" Ram recoils, horror-stricken. "That ain't
right either!"

Clearly, Ram is twitchy about man-to-man contact.

"We didn't know you were married," Zen says, slapping him on the shoulder in a very hetero way that still
makes Ram go rigid. "She told us she was engaged."

"Actually, Zen," I say, slowly hitting on the truth.
"She never *said* she was engaged. I just assumed that she
was engaged because of the way she was dressed when she
showed up here." I turn to Ram. "She made a big deal
about wearing the veil."

I didn't ask enough questions. Or any questions at all,
really. I was too busy thinking about myself, and how her

arrival in my life would mess it up.

"How did you know to find her here anyway?" I ask Ram as gently as possible.

He's quiet for at least a minute before he finally exhales a tremulous breath and says, "Until she found out about you, she didn't have anywhere else to go."

This is not the response I was expecting.

Zen suddenly hops up and says, "I have an idea to help this conversation along!" He bounces over to my parents' fully stocked bar, messes around for a few moments, then comes forward with a short glass of dark liquid. Gah. Somewhere in the African savannah, Ash and Ty's GUARDIAN alarm is going off.

"Take this," Zen says to Ram.

"What is it?" Ram hiccups.

"This," Zen says, holding out the glass, "is a shot of premium aged whiskey. It will help open up your mind." He turns to me and whispers, "And your mouth."

Zen might be a bit of a genius. A light buzz might actually make Ram less self-conscious and more communicative—I mean, I know I'm far more fluent in Mandarin after I've knocked back a few. But the manboy isn't having it.

"Nononono." Ram pinches his mouth and shakes his head.

"Okaaay," Zen says in resignation. "I didn't want to have to give up my stash but . . ." He reaches into his back pocket, pinches a tiny baggie containing a small green pill.

166

"How about this . . . *vitamin*. A vitamin that will make everything feel better!"

That's no vitamin. That's a 10 mg of Tocin!

"I want to feel better," Ram says in a small voice.

Without another word, I yank Zen out of the common room.

"WATCH THE ARM. That arm belongs to the number-one-ranked—"

"Pause it!" I hiss. "Have you gone terminal? What are *you* of all people doing with that stuff anyway? I thought you were all against the, um, chemical manipulation of our most basic animalian instincts or, um, whatever."

Zen talks so much that it's difficult to remember anything that he actually says.

"You're overreacting," he says.

"For serious? *You* were the one to go manifesto on Shoko when *she* was dosing. About how it's totally illegal to hold without a scrip."

Up until now, I thought Zen and I were the only two sophomores at Princeton Day Academy who *hadn't* dosed. It's a popular party drug, way easier to score than beer, weed, or even Oxy. Lib always warned me to stay away from illicit recreational use because he'd seen too many clients breach contracts with amateur bumpings that would have never happened without it.

"If *you* want to get all high and humpy, that's your choice. But who knows how *he'll* react?"

"Have you looked at him?" Zen asks incredulously.

"He's a two-hundred-and-twenty-pound mountain of muscle. That's a tiny dose for a Goliath like him. It'll be enough to make him feel good, but not *too* good."

"I want to feel good," Ram says from the other room.

"Good enough to tell us the truth about that mysterious sister of yours," Zen says. "The one who is out there impersonating you as we sit here and have this debate."

I sigh, knowing this is really our best option for getting any answers out of Ram that will make any sense. Plus, if he gives the Tocin to Ram, he can't take it himself and use it with . . .

Whomever Zen planned to use it with.

"Zen?"

"Yeah?"

"If he tries to impregnate my couch, *you're* cleaning it up."

"You can't be the designated driver as many times as I have and not know how to clean up such messes," Zen replies affably, as if none of this is out of the ordinary. "Besides, that only happens when you crush and snort it."

I don't even want to know how he knows that.

harmony
melody

HIS VOICE—RESONANT AND REASSURING—IS THE FIRST
sound I hear.

"We're here."

I've had my senses shut off for the whole wild ride.
How long we've been chased, I can't say. It might have
been an instant or an eternity.

"Don't worry," he says in his smooth, soothing voice.
"You're with me. I'm a pro."

I'm with Him. That's all I need to hear. There's nothing to fear as long as he's beside me. Ready to know the
unknowable, I slowly open my eyes to see . . .

A parking lot?

"We're at the Avatarcade," he says. "You're into 4-D,
right?"

I shake my head no.

"Really? I thought I read in your file. . . ." He stops himself again. "I went to the first Avatarcade when it opened in Tokyo a few years ago. I'm not so into facespace role-play but it was all the surge on the MiNet and I wanted to see what all the yawping was about. So I go there and guess what? The Jondoe avatar was their top seller! Japan loves me! I had no idea! I've been making major yen off my simulation rights but I didn't even know it. Anyway, I wanted to try out the Jondoe avatar, you know, to see how others experience being me, but they wouldn't let me because there's risk of a permanent schizophrenic split."

I don't even pretend to know what he's saying.

"It's go time," Jondoe says. He hands me a smaller pair of mirrored sunglasses that are otherwise identical to his own. "There will be more of what we had before, so wear these."

I put them on only because he seems to know what's going on and I don't.

"I'll get out and say my lines to the paps. All you have to do is look at me adoringly and smile. Then we'll slip back into the car without going inside. The whole scene will take about a minute, then we'll move on to the next location. The paps all know the deal, we worked it all out in advance. It's all been awesomely staged."

And just when I'm about to beg God for his forgiveness, that I never wanted to be deceitful about my true identity, Jondoe gets out the car and shouts, "Get out of our facespace! We only want to role-play in peace!"

And then he comes around to my side and throws open the door and I'm again bombarded with flashing lights as I was at Melody's house. Only now, through the filtered lenses of the glasses, I can see the truth behind where they're coming from.

"If you scummers don't leave us alone, I'll have to put an end to my charity work!"

I'm not being chased by angels . . .

"Miss Melody Mayflower is just regular girl! She deserves her privacy!"

I'm being chased by the press.

Jondoe rushes to my side and wraps his arms around me. He whispers in my ear, "Give 'em what they want! That's the deal! Or they'll never leave us alone."

Too stunned to think for myself, I look up at him in adoration, smile for the cameras.

I'm blinded by the explosion of flashes. Dazed, I slip back into the car.

Moments later, Jondoe is beside me once again.

"I knew you were a natural," he says, tearing out of the parking lot.

melody
harmony

"I FEEL GOOD," RAM SAYS. "I FEEL BETTER."

Zen nudges me in the shoulder. He's mouthing *"toldja toldja"* and doing a downscaled version of the dance. He's not taking any of this seriously. I reach for another pillow and threaten him with a penalty kick to the manparts. He stops the dance.

"Do you feel like telling us about Harmony?" I ask Ram trepidatiously, pulling the pillow in front of my chest. I don't want him getting any amorous ideas.

He tilts his head to the side. "Sure," he says loosely.

He's already unbuttoned the top button of his shirt, removed the ice helmet and muddy boots. He's now nestling his large frame into the oversize couch cushions, his whole body totally at ease.

"You can start talking now."

He looks genuinely surprised. "Oh, you mean *now*?"

I'm trying my best to be patient, to remind myself that it isn't his fault he's one haybale short of whatever haybales are used for.

"Yes, now."

"All right," he says seemingly unaware of my agitation. "Well, we were all shocked when Harmony told us that she had found an identical twin sister." He stops and dips his head in my direction. "That's you."

I'm smiling so hard my teeth might fall out.

"You look just like her," he says. "Are you *sure* you aren't her?"

I roll my eyes. "Just keep talking."

"Sure," he says genially. "And by the next prayer service, she had the whole settlement praying on you. How thrilling it must have been for you to feel our prayers filling up that God-shaped hole in your soul!"

Unless prayer can be mistaken for the indigestion brought on by too many instant chimichangas, I haven't felt a thing.

"Harmony really, really wanted to witness to you. She felt awful guilty that she had been chosen to live with the Church and that you had been forced to live in sin through no fault of your own. It didn't seem just, especially when it could have just as easily gone the other way round. And the more she talked to you and got to know you, the more she was worried about you living without the Bible out here in Otherside and not having God and suffering in a Jesus-free eternity and all that bad stuff. She became convinced that it was her mission in life to save you from wickedness in this life and the next. Especially when she found out that you were selling your babies."

He says all this without a trace of judginess in his voice. He's simply stating the truth as he sees it.

"Harmony believed that once you met her you would want to move to Goodside, get married, and join our household."

"She really believed that?" Zen asks. "She clearly doesn't know Melody."

"And I certainly don't know Harmony, do I?" I retort.

Ram keeps talking. "That's Harmony, for you. Dedicated to ministering to the unchurched, more than any other girl in our settlement. Especially after the bust-up of her first engagement."

Ooooh. Now we're getting somewhere.

"What happened to the first fiancé anyway?" I ask.

Ram stiffens. "Well, he up and married someone else, one of her other housesisters, actually. The Council prayed on it and decided she wasn't ready. They said Harmony asked too many questions. Too hardheaded and rebellious to husband to. I thought that was a load of goose poop." He pauses. "Until . . ."

Until she ran off without him.

Ram is clearly hurting, and yet he's reluctant to say anything neggy about his wife.

"She had hoped you would come out to see her, but you didn't. When she went missing I knew right away that she had disobeyed the Orders and gone Wayward to see you. I just don't understand why she wanted you to believe she was engaged and not . . . ."

The unsaid "married" just hangs there, suspended by the palpable tension. It's what we all want to know, but none of us can answer. Ram's eyes are getting all watery again, which makes me nervous that maybe the Tocin isn't as powerful as we thought it would be.

"Why would she leave without me?" He tries to smile again. And fails.

I make my best guess. "You're telling us it's against the rules to leave the settlement, right?"

Ram nods. "Except for approved missionary trips or trade, yep. She's Wayward right now for sure. She'll have to wear a red dress when she returns."

"A red dress?" Zen and I ask.

"Red's the color for shunning," Ram says grimly, twisting at his wedding ring.

Shunning? "How long will she be shunned?" This is alarming, to say the least.

"We won't know until the Council prays on it," Ram says. "I got three months when I got caught—" He thrusts a clenched fist to his mouth and squeezes his eyes tight.

Zen and I gape at each other.

Caught doing *what*? What could be so bad to deserve being ignored by your family and friends and everyone you know for three months? It's clear from the panic-stricken expression stretching across Ram's face that there's no way he'll tell us what he got caught doing.

Zen handles this tricky situation with ease.

"If you had gotten in trouble before," Zen says in a very leading way, "I bet Harmony didn't tell you so you wouldn't get in trouble again."

"But I'm her husband, she should have trusted me," he says softly. "It's *my* fault that she couldn't trust me. Something's wrong with *me* . . ."

Maybe Ram was caught with another girl? That would help explain why Harmony was unhappy to marry him.

"How long have you and Harmony been married?" I ask.

He counts off on his fingers. "Three days."

Zen and I both reel back in surprise. "Three days!"

"Three days," he repeats. "Counting today."

"What?" I'm sure I've misunderstood him. "She ran away the day after you got married?"

He nods solemnly, sniffs. "The morning after."

Zen and I exchange the same look, asking the same question: *What happened on the honeymoon?* Only Zen has the nerve to actually ask it out loud.

"What happened?"

The point-blank shot to the heart is too much for Ram to take, even under the cheer-uppy influence of Tocin. He buries his tear-stained face in his hands again.

I look to Zen for help but this time he just shrugs.

After what seems like a full trimester, Ram finally gets himself together. He leans in very close and lowers his voice to a whisper.

"If I tell you something, you promise you can't tell anyone."

"Promise," Zen and I say.

"The truth is, we may not be really married in the eyes of God."

harmony

melody

AFTER WE LEFT THE AVATARCADE, WE SPED THROUGH THE darkness once again and headed to the Underground All-Sports Arena, where an even thicker "scrum of scummers," as Jondoe put it, followed, fotoed, and filmed us as we kicked around a soccer ball for a few minutes. Or rather, Jondoe kicked around a soccer ball and I took a ball to the head, shins, and—at least once, to the shock of the crowd—belly.

Jondoe joked with the paps. "No more of *that* after tonight!"

And now, sitting across from Jondoe while he peruses the menu at the U.S. Buff-A, I'm embarrassed to admit—even to myself—that I had thought—if only briefly—the Rapture had arrived. I know Jondoe would mock me mistaking camera flashes for the Apocalypse. But that's only because Othersiders like him don't fret nearly as much about End Times as Goodsiders like me do.

Or did.

"She'll have the West Virginia pepperoni-roll appetizer and the New Mexican Tacos Supremos as her entrée," Jondoe says to the waitress. Then to me, "I know it's your favorite."

I manage a feeble smile. I don't know how he can act so normal with so many eyes on us.

"And I'll have the eastern seaboard seafood special. Grilled, not fried," he says, patting his abdominals. "Gotta stay fit, you know." Then he hands the menus over to the waitress, who takes them as if she were Moses receiving the Ten Commandments.

There are dozens of eyes on us in the restaurant. And thousands, maybe even millions, more watching live on the MiNet. The small crowd has kept a respectful distance so far, until two girls break rank and flutter over to our table. With their reddish blond hair, full-moon faces, and slightly slanted eyes, they remind me of my housesister Annie, whose unusual beauty always caused her so much worry until she married Shep.

"I'm your biggest fan," says the older sister, who is wearing a Princeton University sweatshirt.

"My sister wants me to bump with you," says the younger girl, fiddling with the strap on her First Curse Purse.

The older sister steps directly in front of her. "I think you two would make me the most beautiful mixmatchy pregg. It's never too early to plan these things, is it?"

Jondoe smiles weakly, reaches into his front pocket, hands her a business card. "Contact my agent." Then he tugs on his ear. Within seconds, two bear-size men in black drag the two girls away.

"Oh my grace!" I cry as the girls struggle to free themselves. "Are they going to be okay?"

"Don't worry," Jondoe says. "They're on my security detail. It always gets a little mobby whenever I'm paired up for a new pregg."

Roughly twenty-five yards away, his security team has cordoned off the opposite corner of the restaurant for the gathering crowd of curious onlookers. We're sitting at a booth in Hawaii. They're kept all the way across the floor map in Maine.

"So." Jondoe returns his attention to me as if none of this has just happened. "What were we talking about?"

Nothing. And that's because I've barely uttered a word since we left Melody's house.

"You're upset about those two humpers, aren't you?" he says.

I nod.

"I'm not here to make any side deals," he says reassuringly. "When my agent found out I was coming to town, she tried to hook me into being a ringer at a University Bump-a-thon being held tonight at one of the campus eating clubs." He gives me a reassuring look. "I told her to delete herself. That kind of mass insemination is something you do at the start of your career, or at the end, not in your prime. So she put Phoenix on booty duty, not me. He's a good guy, but he just turned eighteen, which is a major bonerkiller, right? I mean, none of us know *exactly* when our systems will shut down, but he's lucky if he's got another year in him before he's forced to retire."

The waitress returns. She carelessly plunks my soda down, the drink spilling over the side and into my lap. Then with no small measure of ceremony, she very deliberately leans over the table as she sets down Jondoe's bottle, providing us both with a clear view of that which we should not be able to see. "I'm peaking," she whispers before walking away.

Jondoe keeps talking, seemingly unaware of our waitress's flirtations.

"This town is full of girls who put their virginity on lockdown because they think they're better than everyone else. Why settle when there's always a better deal right around the corner? These Eggs are priceless, right? So they pass and pass and pass and then they're eighteen-year-old freshgirls and suddenly find themselves with no prospects for continuing their precious bloodline because all the smart Sperm have already hedged their bets on less discerning fourteen-year-olds. So their parents are losing their minds because they don't want this to be the end of the family line, so these prissy freshgirls get so failful that they end up bumping with the first loser splooger that comes—ha, *comes*—their way. Or, in the case of the girls at the Bump-a-thon, they end up spending money to *hire* a professional when they should have been making money *as* a professional. Either way is a poor investment strategy. Surrogettes like you have gamed the system, and for that I raise my bottle."

Jondoe holds up his bottle of Potent Pale Ale for the press to see before taking a long draft. "Making great nights last even longer!" He delivers the line with hearty cheer.

I fold my hands and say a silent prayer over my soda. *Bless this beverage, Lord. And please let it not be tampered with by demonic forces of envy and evil. Amen.*

I sip my glass of Coke '99 quietly. It's too sweet and the bubbles tickle the inside of my nose, but I don't want to trouble the devilish waitress by asking for a drink of water any more than my mere presence with Jondoe in this booth already has.

"With your reproaesthetical looks, you'll cash in on endorsements," he says, winking left, winking right, then blinking a few quick times in succession before winking once more. "It's a major revenue stream. . . ."

"Mmm."

It's the only thing I can say.

Then, without a word, Jondoe holds his bottle out to me. A trickle drips down the side of the bottle, like the sweat I can feel tickling against my own skin.

He knows what I need without even asking

Jondoe presses the bottle up to my parted lips and I drink greedily, as hundreds, thousands, millions of eyes watch.

melody
harmony

NOW, THIS IS TOO MUCH FOR ME TO TAKE.

"What do you mean you may not really be married? Did you say your vows or not?"

"We did! But . . ."

"BUT WHAT?"

"We didn't, you know." Ram looks away shyly. *"Consummate."*

I let this sink in for a moment. Zen makes an immature simulation of coitus with his fingers.

"You mean you never . . ."

"NO!" Ram shouts, eyes squeezed tight, face burning red. "Or. Yes. I mean, sort of."

"Let me guess," Zen says. "Misplaced payload."

Ram hangs his head, neither confirming nor denying Zen's accusation.

"What does the Pro/Am call it when a guy finishes before he begins? Ejaculatory genocide?"

DELETE MY BRAIN CACHE, PLEASE.

I know they're married and naked activities are a natural part of honeymooning and all, but hearing this about Ram and my sister is making me gag. This doesn't escape Zen's notice.

"For a Surrogette, you are for seriously repressed about sex."

"Am not."

"You do realize that *this*"—Zen makes the porny gesture again—"is how preggs are made, right? Or are you hoping that science comes up with a viable form of Artificial Biological Conception just in time for you to bump?"

The physical act of pregging is not something I spend a lot of time thinking about. But that doesn't mean I'm repressed. It just means that my parents have seen to it that I'm too overscheduled to think about such things.

"I think I need to get right with myself," Ram says out of nowhere.

"Okay," we say.

Ram fills his chest with air, opens his mouth—and two hysterical voices fill the room instead.

"WHAT IS GOING ON, PELL-MEL?"

harmony
melody

JONDOE WAVES HIS HANDS IN FRONT OF MY FACE. "WHERE ARE you, Miss Melody Mayflower?"

I startle at the sound of his voice. I look up and catch a glimpse of her face—my face—in the mirror on the wall directly in front of our booth.

I am Miss Melody Mayflower.

A cheese-covered lump is getting cold sitting on the platter in front of me, untouched. I hadn't even noticed the arrival of my entrée.

"I'm here," I say, feeling not very here at all.

"*You* were hypnotized by something unlookawayable, that's for sure. Maybe a few dozen messages from a certain top-five trender on the MiNet?"

"I'm not on the MiNet," I reply. The words come out

easily. A few sips from his bottle have loosened my tongue. The longer I'm with him, the more myself I feel. Even as I pretend to be someone I'm not. I'd be confused by this if I weren't so . . . content.

"Why haven't you replied to any of the links I sent you?" he asks, squeezing lemon onto his fillet.

"I wasn't on the MiNet."

He can't stop smiling. "I wanted to be the one to warn you that there's a lot of scum out there about me."

He turns in the booth and makes a point of staring down the paparazzi still "respecting our privacy" from across the restaurant. The crowd is getting rowdier now, with the press being outnumbered by girls waving hand-made signs that say things like: PICK ME! I'M PEAKING! Or: MAKE MY PREGG! They're held back by a half-dozen senti-nels on Jondoe's security team, all of whom look like they could easily tote a cow under each arm. I wonder if they've taken that HGH that Zen told me about. If so, they must have very small brains. The Bible says that a wise man is better than a strong man, but an army of wise men would not be able to keep these peaking, shrieking girls away from what they want.

And what they want is Jondoe.

"I'm not on the MiNet," I repeat, before remembering who I'm supposed to be and quickly adding, "right now."

"Really?" he asks, slightly deflated. "It's fine if you don't want to follow me. But aren't you the least bit curi-ous about public opinion? Don't you want to know what the MiNet is saying about you?"

"About me?"

"Yes, you," he says with a laugh. "There are a lot of eyeballs on you right now. You're trending in the top ten. Everyone wants to know all about Melody Mayflower, the 'regular girl' bumping with the hottest RePro. . . ."

"I LOVE YOU, JONDOE!" shouts a voice in the crowd.

"ME TOO!" screams another.

I suddenly feel very queasy. My West Virginia pepperoni-roll appetizer is spinning in my stomach.

Jondoe acts as if he can't hear the commotion we're causing. "More than ninety percent of my followers think that we'll create the hottest pregg since I bumped with Miss Teen Venezuela. . . ."

"PREGG ME!"

"You might want to watch your language, though," he says. "When you said, 'Oh my grace!' your poll numbers shot up in the Bible Belt, but dipped on both coasts. . . ."

"You were reading about me?" I shiver involuntarily. "This whole time?"

"Hell yeah," he says. He reaches out to touch my braid. "Girls in the six-to-twelve demo really like your hair that way."

At some point I had twisted the plait back together again. A nervous habit.

"And I'm not just reading, but watching the live streams as they happen, so I can see us as they do," he says. "And we look like we'll make one hot bump."

Hysterical screams now. It reminds me of the primal panic of livestock on the way to the slaughterhouse. Only I feel like the doomed animal.

Jondoe and I lock eyes and express the same thought at the same time.

"We need to get out of here."

Our voices coming together make the sweetest music in my soul, a respite amid the chaos.

He tugs on his ear and two out of six bodyguards leave their posts to escort us out of the restaurant. I fear for the safety of the four bodyguards left behind.

"NO! DON'T GO!"

And then it happens: The adoring throng has turned into an angry mob. The girls push forward in a frenzied stampede that will trample anyone that stands in its way.

"JONDOE!"

I am the obstacle between what they want, and what they cannot have.

Jondoe assertively wraps his body around me, a human shield against this animal crush. And right then, in the middle of the desperate scuttle out the emergency exit to safety, he whispers soothingly and so quietly that I shouldn't be able to hear it over the delirious din but I do.

"Melody . . . Melody . . . Melody . . ."

And even though it's me who Jondoe is protecting and not her, not my own twin, the one who has been waiting for him for years, I am overtaken by the raging sin of jealousy. I am the sisters. I am the waitress. I am the girls who are now punching and kicking and raging at the locks on the opposite side of the emergency exit, because I hate hearing him say so tenderly, so lovingly, the name of this girl Melody who is not me.

I need to tell Jondoe the truth about who I am.

I need to hear him say *my* name.

melody
harmony

"WHAT IS GOING ON HERE?"

Ash and Ty are more ectopic than usual because they think *I'm* the one boozing from their liquor cabinet.

"GET IN THE 2VU WHERE WE CAN SEE YOU RIGHT NOW."

"Don't move," I say, before checking to make sure that the couch is just out of view. One look at Ram and my parents would be convinced that I'm up for Churchy indoctrination. "You stay out of view too," I warn Zen, just for good measure. My parents don't have anything against Zen personally. They simply regard him with the same wary suspicion that they regard every other male between the ages of twelve and obsolescence, as a threat against everything they've worked toward for the past sixteen years.

My parents are still screaming at each other, their eyes practically popping off their faces. "SHE HACKED THE SYSTEM!"

I press the 2Vu. "Who hacked what system?"

My parents quiet at the sight of me.

"You're home," Ash says.

"Just like the stalk app said you were," Ty says.

"The whole time . . ."

"Right," I say. "I came home straight after my Pro/Am meeting today and haven't left the house since. Look, I'm sorry about the—"

"But you're all over the MiNet!" Ash says, not letting me finish my bogus apology about the missing booze. "At the Underground All-Sports Arena, the Avatarcade—"

"You caused a riot at the U.S. Buff-A on Route One," Ty breaks in. "A dozen girls got stungunned!"

I hear a curious "Huh?" coming from direction of the couch. I glance over to see Zen's eyes winking and blinking furiously.

"Why didn't you tell us you were bumping with the highest-ranked RePro in the history of the Standards?"

"Why didn't you tell us all our financial problems are solved?"

Wow. And I thought my parents were dosed when I talked to them this morning. I *told* them to lay off the Tocin brownies.

"You're getting very high approval ratings, Melody, just as we always knew you would!"

"But you could try harder to win over the thirteen-to-seventeen demo, who are jealous that you're bumping with Jondoe and they're not—"

"Who?" I ask. "What?"

"Jondoe," says Zen, coming toward me, a stunned expression on his face.

"And to think that we were *this close* to going off contract and setting up a sub-rosa spermination . . ."

Zen steps between me and my parents on the MiVu.

"Hey, Ash!" He waves spastically at the screen. "Hi, Ty!"

Oh, no. He's put on the synthetically chipper voice that he uses whenever he's in major neg, which doesn't happen all that often and is doubly worrisome when it does.

"Congratulations! You've waited so long and worked so hard to see Melody reach the tip-top of her profession, and must be so proud of yourselves. You deserve a reward! Now go out and party your parental asses off! Starting right now!"

He blinks off the MiVu and then, on second thought, removes the whole system from the powergrid.

"What was *that* all about?"

He turns back to me, puts both hands on my shoulders, and gives me a sobering look.

"You need to MiNet yourself right now."

"Why? What's going on?"

"Just do it."

My eyes can't move fast enough. When I log on to the

MiNet, I see that I've got thousands of new followers sending me thousands of new messages. They're easy to read, though, because most of them ask variations of the same question:

JONDOE WTF?

At this point, I'm wondering the same thing myself.

"Why am I getting spamslammed about Jondoe?"

"Look at the links I just sent you!"

I open Zen's links. And there, before my very eyes, is foto after foto of me with the hottest RePro on the MiNet.

There's me and Jondoe splitting a West Virginia pepperoni roll at the U.S. Buff-A. There's me and Jondoe kicking the ball around at the Underground All-Sports Arena. There's me and Jondoe standing beside a car in the parking lot of the Avatarcade. Finally, a grainy shot of me and Jondoe standing in front of the window in my bedroom . . .

"Who would go to such trouble to fotobomb me?" I ask.

"No one fotobombed you, Mel."

Zen sends a video. I recognize the setting right away as the parking lot to the U.S. Buff-A on Route 1. Jondoe has an arm around my (my!) waist and is addressing the crowd of gawkers. The audio quality is pretty pissy, even after I adjust the volume on my earbuds.

"Melody and I both just want to thank our Repro Reps—Lib from UGenXX Talent Agency, and Stella from Exceptional Conceptional Management—for making the deal," he says. "We can't wait to start working together."

I blink it off. I can't watch any more, now that I've finally grasped what was so obvious to Zen.

I wasn't fotobombed. The footage is real, but it's not me posing next to Jondoe. . . .

"She counterfeited me."

harmony
melody

WE'RE HURTLING OVER THE HILLS AT A HUNDRED MILES PER hour.

"Whoa," he says. "That was pretty intense. But it was worth it, right?"

I don't think I've exhaled since we got in the car.

"We're done with promo for the night. The paps got more than they needed, so they'll leave us alone now," he says. "It doesn't help any of us to get too overexposed too soon. The asking price of their footage goes down. And our value is subject to backlash fluctuations. . . ."

None of this means anything to me. "Where are we?"

"Not too far from the last stop on our . . . *date*."

He wants me to ask where we're going so he can refuse to tell me. Don't ask me how I know this. I just do. I *know* him. I know him better than I know my own husband, and we were in diapers together. Jondoe is totally focused on me, which would be glorious if it didn't mean he wasn't paying any attention at all to the road. The car directly in front of us is flashing its brake lights.

"Watch out!"

He jumps, looks behind him. "For what?"

"The car!" But before I've even said it, our car slows down to avoid a collision.

He gives me a curious look. "I've got it on Autodrive," he says slowly, cautiously, the equivalent to tiptoeing around a field to avoid cow patties.

"Autodrive," I say. "Right. Of course."

Our settlement shares a garage of cars and trucks, all of which are at least thirty years old and don't have the modern amenities commonly found in Othersiders' personal transport. Gas-powered putterers are just fine when your whole world exists within a few square miles. No one is ever in a real hurry to go anywhere when there's nowhere to go.

"I don't have a car like this," I say, hoping this might provide a logical opening for me to tell him the truth. "Because . . . well . . . you see . . ."

He nods in acknowledgment. "You ride a bike to school because you're the president of the ECOmmunity Club. I read that."

Melody's file.

I am fascinated by Melody's file. As much as I want

197

Jondoe to know who I am, I want to know who my twin is even more.

"What else does my file say about me?"

"It's your file." He gives me a blank look. "You already know it."

I think fast. "I want to hear it from you."

"You want to hear about the file that told me that you don't like flowers but love Coke '99 and GlycoGoGo Bars."

Yes. I nod for him to keep going.

"And told me you were a varsity soccer star and didn't allow a single goal before your team had to forfeit the rest of the season. Your favorite player on the National Team is number fifteen. You play real guitar, not guitarbot, are far above average in intelligence, and plan to apply to the Global University, where you will pursue a career in epidemiology. Your personal heroes are the international team of scientists who found a cure for HIV and you'd like to be on the team that either finds a cure for the Virus or develops a viable form of petri-pregging, maybe through, um, embryonic stem-cell research or something called partial reproductive organ transplantation—whatever any of that even means." He raises an eyebrow. "You're aware that all of this would put us out of business, right?"

I'm learning more about my sister from this file than I've heard from her. I get so caught up in my silent prayers of gratitude that I almost miss what he says next.

"Your birthparents are unknown, you were abandoned

at a hospital when you were just a few hours old and adopted a few weeks later."

I can barely eke out a whisper. "You know that?"

"If it's in your file, I know it," he says. "You're lucky you didn't try to become a Surrogette twenty years ago before the YDNA tests could prove your Northern European ancestry within one one-hundred-thousandth of a percentage point. The Jaydens would've never signed a contract without it. Anyone willing to take a chance on a total unknown might as well save money and make a postdelivery bid on an amateur." He pauses, puts on a meditative face. "Then again, it wasn't legal to pay teens to bump back then. But I guess that's because there wasn't the supply-and-demand issue that there is now, you know, until a bunch of brains like you find a cure for the Virus—"

Then car slams the brakes so suddenly that I'm thrown toward the dashboard. I'm wearing my seat belt, but Jondoe throws a protective arm over me anyway.

"HEY, JACK-OFF. TRY AUTODRIVE," Jondoe yells to the driver of the car that cut into our lane. "Sorry about that," he says, though he doesn't seem sorry at all to have a reason to keep his hand resting across my lap.

We blur past a few dozen streetlights before I finally will myself to speak. "The file."

"Right," Jondoe says as the car slows down and turns onto a narrow path. "It said that you wanted to book a room at the only MiNet-blinded accommodations in the county."

He points out the window toward a sign: WELCOME TO THE INN IN THE WOODS: DISCONNECT TO RECONNECT.

"Surprise! I didn't put that on the itinerary because I didn't want it to get leaked to the press," he says. "I know you don't want any distractions when we get down to business."

Get down to business?

"It's your first time," he says. "You're nervous. I understand." He reaches into his knapsack, takes out a small bottle of pills, shakes it. "Tocin will help you open up."

Open up?

"And I'm not just saying that because I'm a paid spokesperson," he says. "It will be fun. Satisfaction guaranteed."

Satisfaction? Guaranteed?

"I know it's hard for you to believe, but I was a virgin once."

I back myself up against the car door and blurt, "What's *your* story?"

At first he looks alarmed, but then his features soften into something else. Amusement maybe.

"My story?"

"Why do you do . . . *this*?"

He closes his eyes, rubs the golden hairs on his chin. When he finally speaks, it's in a voice much quieter, yet even more commanding than before.

"The answer isn't in my file, is it?"

Of course I haven't the faintest idea what's in Jondoe's file, but I don't let on.

"I've been subjected to more physical and mental evaluations than I ever thought possible. I've done the YDNA, of course. VO$_2$ max, flexibility, and isoinertial strength assessments. Myers-Briggs, Winfrey-McGraw . . ."

He smiles ruefully.

"And?"

He looks up, right into my eyes. "And no one has ever asked me that question. Not once. They just . . . assume."

"Who assumes what?"

"Everyone assumes I do it to *do it*." He rolls his eyes, laughs. "For the sex."

I feel my cheeks burning. "Y-y-you don't?"

"No," he says dismissively. "With so many girls waiting to be bumped, just about any guy can get some ass anytime."

I flinch at his coarse language, then think of Melody's friend Zen, who would offer an altogether different opinion on the subject.

"It's not the money either. Though it definitely doesn't suck getting paid to do something I would do for free." His eyes dart toward the window. "And I know you won't believe me, but it's not about the fame-gaming."

"Then why *do* you do it?"

"It's really not about me at all. It's about . . ." He falls back onto the headrest and looks up through the moon-roof. "I'm providing a valuable service." Unhappy with his explanation, he screws up his perfect face and tries again.

"No. It's more like . . ." He stops himself once more. "I want to do good. That's why I accepted the Jaydens' application."

"I don't understand."

"Oh, come on," he says. "The Jaydens do okay for themselves, but they weren't anywhere near affluential enough to meet my minimum bid. It just so happens that I am very passionate about helping aspirational couples who want an upmarket pregg. So once a year I do some pro boner work and the Jaydens are this year's pick."

"That's very generous of you."

"If you had something that could change people's lives for the better, wouldn't you want them to have it?"

I suppose I would.

"Such an extraordinary gift is meant to be shared."

It is, isn't it?

"I figure that if I was put on this earth to do this one thing, I should do it to the very best of my ability for however long as I'm equipped to do so."

Yes!

"I feel exactly the same way!" I say.

"About delivering a pregg?"

"No!" I cry, my heart beating madly. "About spreading the Word of God!"

Oh my grace! I just couldn't stop myself! The spirit moved me to tell the Truth. I'm ready for Jondoe to call me a freak, kick me out of the car, and dash away faster than an unbroken pony.

But he doesn't.

"You're a surprising girl, Miss Melody Mayflower," he says. "So encrypted."

My cheeks are roaring now, I can feel it.

"I've been in the business for three years now," he says. "I showed up here today thinking I knew everything I needed to know about you to make this transaction go as smoothly as possible. But . . ."

He leans back, looks me over. If I could show him all of me, my soul, my everything, I would. I *will*. It's time to make my confession.

"I'm not the girl in the file!"

Jondoe doesn't hesitate. "I'm not who I am in my file either."

"You're not?"

Even though there's just the two of us together in his car, he motions for me to come closer. My flesh goose bumps at the warmth of his whisper on my neck.

"Jondoe obviously isn't my real name. That's just the name my agent at ECM gave me because she thought it would be better for my man brand. I've never told a Surrogette my real name. But you, Miss Melody Mayflower, are no ordinary Surrogette. You're special. Do you want to know my real name?"

"I want to know everything."

And not just in the spiritual sense of knowing him in my heart, but the physical, tangible sense of knowing him, a knowing that lets me reach out and touch his hands, as he touched me moments ago.

"Then let me take you somewhere else that isn't on the itinerary," he says.

I tell him I'm ready to be taken.

REBIRTH

Push it out or pull it out
Ain't nuttin' to worry 'bout.
                    —Fed Double X, "Bumpin'"

harmony
melody

I OPEN MY EYES TO SEE THE MAN WHO HAS WALKED BESIDE
me in my dreams for as long as I can remember dreaming.

"Wake up," Jondoe says.

I unstick my cheek from the window, dislodge my
tongue from the roof of my mouth, wipe the sleep out of
my eyes.

"How long was I asleep?"

"Not long." Then he looks as if he's about to add something, then reconsiders.

"What?" I ask.

"What *what*?"

"You looked like you were about to say something. . . ."

He lowers his chin, looks up at me through his lashes.

"You talk in your sleep."

My cheeks burn. How shameful for him to know this about me.

"Now, now," he says, patting me on the back, "Don't be embarrassed. You didn't say anything too incriminating. . . ."

"No man has ever heard me talking in my sleep!" I say. "Not even my h—"

I should have just come out and said it. Husband. Not even my husband.

"Who?" Jondoe asks.

"No one," I reply.

I think about Ram. I hope he hasn't come looking for me. I pray he uses this time apart to recognize that he'll never be able to hold up his side of the marital quadrangle: God, man, woman, child(ren). I know this, our parents know this, and the Church Council knew it when they put us—two unteachable spirits—together. If he finally accepts the truth about himself, then I'll know I did him a favor by leaving. I only wish I'd had the courage to do it before the wedding.

Ma remembers the last horse-and-buggy days and the arrival of the first truck. "A Dodge *Ram*," she likes to remind me, as if this alone would make him the ideal husband. Ma has seen how Orders are made and Orders are unmade as mere men interpret God's Word one way and then change their interpretations to see it another, altogether different way. Maybe one day I'll tell my daughter about how I had to wear veils and dresses that fell to my ankles and she, in her T-shirts and jeans, won't believe me. Maybe I'll tell my daughter about having to marry a man I didn't love, and how lucky she is that she grew up in a different time.

If I have a daughter.

If I ever go back.

"Let's do this," Jondoe says, opening the car door.

I get out of the car and make note of our surroundings for the first time. We're parked in the circular driveway of a two-story house that sits on the wide corner lot of a block lined up with near-identical homes. The large, boxy structure doesn't look all that different from our houses in Goodside. True, the front and side yards aren't cultivated with any plants worth growing—it's three-quarters of an acre of wasted greenspace. And there's a detached garage where a barn should be. Otherwise, this vinyl-sided house with the stone facade is in keeping with the outsize suburban fashion of the early to mid '00s. Just like ours—only we fill our houses with four families instead of just one.

A lamp turns on in the downstairs window. Someone knows we're here.

"I haven't been back here in almost a year," Jondoe says.

"Where is here?" I ask.

"Where Gabriel spent the first fourteen years of his life."

Gabriel. Like the angelic messenger sent by Jesus to work on His behalf.

The front door swings open and a man and a woman step out onto the front porch. They're both wearing robes over pajamas, bedroom slippers, and big, toothy grins.

"Gabriel!" they cry out, arms outstretched.

"Who are they?" I ask.

"Gabriel's parents," Jondoe says as he takes the first steps toward them.

I point at him. "Gabriel?"

He says nothing, answering instead with a smile brighter than all the shining lights in the heavens.

melody
harmony

I AM QUITE LITERALLY FLOORED, PARALYZED BY THE NEWS that my married, trubie twin sister spermjacked my RePro, not just any RePro, but the hottest on the MiNet. Which meant that if she *hadn't* showed up on my doorstep, *I* might have already bumped with the hottest RePro on the MiNet.

If that's not enough to floor a girl, I don't know what is.

I have stared at his fotos for . . . I don't know? Hours? Weeks? Aeons? His is an unlookawayable face. Jondoe's face defies any improvements made by the attractiveness app. No tweaking of the distance between his chin and lips, forehead and the bridge of his nose, or between the eyes. The geometry of his face is scientifically perfect. And don't even get me started on his abdominal muscles, which are a study in anatomical symmetry.

I'm supposed to bump with *him*?

Or *was*.

Finally, after whatever amount of time it was, Zen speaks up.

"If Jondoe thinks he's with you," Zen says, "he's probably been messaging you this whole time."

I gasp, knowing that Jondoe *has* been messaging me this whole time . . . only I thought it was spam! I double-blink-wink-left-right-left-blink to read the rest of Jondoe's messages.

Amid all the flattering messages about how reproaesthetical I am, I got an itinerary that matches up with what I saw in the fotos:

Avatarcade

Underground All-Sports Arena

U.S. Buff-A

Surprise!

Then Jondoe spammed me with a bunch of flattering feeds about . . . himself.

But it's the last few messages that made no sense at all:

PSALM 127:3

PSALM 128:3

PSALM 37:5

If Harmony told him that *I* have God, why would *Jondoe* send *me* psalms? Unless, maybe, he was trying to impress her . . .

"Ram! What are the Psalms?"

He thinks for a moment, scratching his head. "Bible verses."

I am dangerously close to throwing a clot.

"Even *I* know that!" I snap. "But what *are* they?"

I don't even wait for Ram to say "don't know" or Zen to look up the passages before messaging Jondoe back. The whole time he's been with Harmony, he thought he was with me. And now he thinks *I* have God! She converted me behind my back. I waste no time in updating my status.

THIS IS THE REAL MELODY

"Psalm one hundred twenty-seven, verse three," Zen reads from the quikiwiki. "'Don't you see that children are God's best gift? The fruit of the womb his greatest legacy?'"

U R WITH MY GODFREAKY TWIN SISTER

"Psalm one hundred twenty-eight, verse three," Zen continues. "'You will bear children as a vine bears grapes.'"

ASK WHAT HER REAL NAME IS

"Psalm thirty-seven, verse five. 'Open up before God, keep nothing back; He'll do whatever needs to be done.'"

TELL HER I'M FOR SERIOUSLY PISSED

A second goes by. Five. Ten.

"That's some righteous versin' right there," Ram says.

Nothing.

"It looks like Jondoe changed his strategy," Zen says, trying to lighten the mood, "from humpy to thumpy."

I. Am. Beyond.

"TERMINATE! NOW! SERIOUSLY!"

I don't need to say it twice. Zen and Ram disappear into the kitchen.

WTF?

Another second goes by. Five. Ten.

I check his location on the MiStalk but he's nowhere to be found. No surprise. He's either blinded himself or has gone off the grid.

WHERE R U?

WHERE R U?

WHERE R U?

harmony
melody

THE SOBBING, HEAVING COUPLE IS HUGGING JONDOE (GABRIEL!)
with no signs of ever letting go. The emotional embrace
that began outside on the front porch has danced itself
inside to the entrance hall.

"It's been so long!"

"Too long!"

I'm uncomfortable watching this reunion.

I've never shared a group hug with my parents. It's just
not appropriate. Church folk don't glorify displays of affections, choosing to support each other through shared labor
rather than shared embraces. My father was remote even
by Church standards and was always far more interested in
my housebrothers than me. Occasionally he gave me pats
on the head, but only when I was much younger and after

I had made myself useful by cleaning the chicken coops. I'm not sad that he never hugged me because that's just the way it was.

My most intimate moments with my mother were also when I was much younger, when I sat in her lap as she braided my hair. Those mornings are the only times I can say her affections were fully focused on me and me alone. She would hum hymns to herself as she smoothed and straightened and plaited my hair, but her fingers were too deft for my liking. Her one-on-one attention never lasted more than a few short minutes before my next housesister was in her lap. I know it's wicked, but I often tied knots into my hair just so Ma would need extra time to comb them out. I don't remember the pain of having my hair pulled into submission, just happiness that I would get to hear Ma hum a whole hymn.

Jondoe's parents haven't noticed my presence, or likelier, they don't care. Even though it's the middle of the night, they are overjoyed beyond words by Jondoe's surprise arrival, barely communicating through undecipherable keening punctuated by the occasional semicomprehensible word burst.

"Gabey! It's you! It's really you!"

"My boy! I can't believe it!"

Jondoe is more object than participant, at one point going out of his way to wink at me over his mother's fluffy pink shoulder, to let me know that he at least remembers that I'm still here.

Motivated more by a need for a distraction than genuine curiosity, my eyes are drawn to one of several small wooden signs mounted by the front door.

GET AN AFTERLIFE!

I quickly read some the other plaques adorning the walls.

THIS HOUSE IS PRAYER–CONDITIONED!

AMERICA NEEDS A FAITH LIFT!

I've never seen so many forms of idolatry in one place! And we've barely gotten through the front door! As a contrast to the humorous exclamatory plaques, there are other more serious displays of faith: A foot-long wooden cross, a large mirror etched with an image of the Last Supper, an ichthus symbol. The Church and other plain sects strictly prohibit any such objects of worship. Crosses and other symbols or artistic representations of passages from the Bible are all too showy. I know these things exist, and that many devout Christians consider such displays a way of being bold for God. But I never, ever expected to see such things in *this* house. . . .

Oh my grace! Could it be?

"Praise the Lord!" chorus his father and mother.

Jondoe's parents have God!

melody
harmony

FOR ALMOST TWO YEARS I WAITED.

I kept my eye on the purity prize. I said no to Tocin.
I stayed on the sidelines during group gropes, or stayed
home and missed the masSEX parties altogether. I turned
down offers from unaccredited worms and free-agent
Sperms until they stopped asking. I watched amateurs turn
into pros, accidents into possibilities. I watched my MiNet
status fall from the "six-figure Surrogette" to a "virge on
the verge." I resisted the pressure to get an everythingbut. I
strenuously avoided touching any member of the opposite
sex, refusing so much as even a first kiss in the fear that any
accidental skin-to-skin contact could—

A warm hand brushes my waist and I nearly leap across
the room.

"AHHHH!"

"Dose down," Zen says. "Get Lib on the MiVu! He's got too much at stake in this to just let the whole deal fall apart, right?"

I nod mutely.

Zen is in his element now. This is where he excels: crisis management.

"Only Lib can tell you when Jondoe signed up with the Jaydens," he says. "Only he can explain why you didn't get the news and how Harmony wound up being your doppelbanger."

I call up Lib on the MiVu.

"LIIIIIIIIIIIB," I shout. "WHEREVER YOU ARE. GET IN VIEW RIGHT NOW."

I stare at his icon, willing it to animate already.

"LIIIIIIIIIIIB," I call out, yanking Zen in front of me. "I'M IN CRISIS. I'M ABOUT TO BUMP WITH A FIVE-FOOT CHINO-CHICANO."

Zen doesn't know whether to be flattered or insulted. "Five foot *eight*."

I shoot him a look.

"Five foot seven and *a half*," he huffs.

I drag Ram into view. "FOR SERIOUS, LIB. I'M GONNA ORGY WITH AN ILLITERATE AGRI-CULTY UNLESS YOU TRY TO STOP ME. . . ."

In an instant, Lib's frozen icon comes to life, or as much life is possible when 95 percent of your face is made from synthetic skinfeel. He starts raving and doesn't stop.

219

"WHY are you threatening the man who made you the hottest Surrogette on the MiNet? WHY haven't you responded to any of my messages, gorgeous? I've been TERMINAL over here. How many hours has it been since insemination? Is it time to piss on the stick? I've already written the press release. It's fertilicious. Knowing Jondoe, I bet you bumped it out on the first try! Though I certainly wouldn't blame you, Miss Melody Mayflower, if you wanted a few do-overs."

It's only when he notices that I've got my arms around Zen and Ram that he breaks from his tirade. His eyes narrow as narrowly as his surgeries will allow.

"Who are these two . . . wor—?" He stops short of calling them "worms."

"Oh, these two?" I say with feigned casualness. "They're my top prospects for going amateur."

Zen and Ram tense up on either side of me.

"WHAT?" Lib mops his sweaty brow with the back of his hand. "Where is JONDOE?"

"I have no idea where Jondoe is," I say. "I never met Jondoe, Lib. I didn't know he had signed with the Jaydens until I saw the news."

Lib laughs high and hysterically. "You're scamming me."

"No, I'm not," I say.

And that's when Lib loses it.

"I SET IT ALL UP WITH YOU THIS MORN-ING," he yells. "I SAW THE FOOTAGE. YOU AND

JONDOE AT THE HOUSE, THE AVATARCADE, THE ALL-SPORTS ARENA, THE U.S. BUFF-A. *EVERYONE HAS!*"

"It wasn't *me*, Lib," I say, leaving it to him to figure out the rest.

His perma-tan pales as much as such artificially tinted synthetic skinfeel can pale, as he suddenly grasps the truth.

"I spoke to *her* this morning?" His voice is barely audible.

"My twin," I whisper. "The only flaw in my file."

harmony

melody

THE THREESOME BREAKS APART. HIS PARENTS' FACES ARE wet and shining with tears of joy. Jondoe is smiling but his eyes are dry.

"It's okay that I came home without telling you first?" Jondoe says, knowing the answer already.

His father looks up at him with adoration and says, "'My son, you are always with me, and everything I have is yours.'"

He couldn't have chosen a more appropriate passage.

"The parable of the lost son," I say in appreciation.

And for the first time, Jondoe's parents have pulled their attention away from Jondoe and are gazing upon me with more than mere interest. Awe.

"Mom and Dad, this is Melody," Jondoe says.

His parents pull me into their group hug with no time

to make room for the Holy Spirit between us. My mouth smashes up against Jondoe's collarbone, my bosom presses against his torso. I let lose a little squeak of shock.

"We're crushing the poor girl!" his mother exclaims as she loosens her grip on me without letting go entirely.

"I'm fine." I realize that I don't know Jondoe's last name. "Mrs. . . . ?"

This question inspires orchestral laughter from parents and son.

"Mrs.?" His mother whoops when she finally catches her breath. "No need for such formalities! Please call me Shelby!"

Shelby has her son's fair hair and skin. Or *he* has *hers*, I suppose. Despite it being the middle of the night, her pretty features pop with more makeup than all the women of Goodside will ever use in their entire lives: slick pink lips to match her bathrobe, thick black lashes, a golden shimmer across her cheekbones.

"And I'm Jake."

His father is a faded version of Jondoe, which is to say that there is a handsome paternal resemblance—warm brown eyes, elastic expressive mouth, strong jaw—and yet he still lacks that mesmerizing quality that makes Jondoe so . . . How did he put it? *Unlookawayable.*

"Thank you," I say, then to be polite, "I was admiring your . . ." I stop myself from saying "idolatry." "Decor."

"We truly believe that a joyful heart is good medicine," says Jake.

I identify the passage automatically. "Proverbs."

His parents gape at each other, then Jondoe.

"She's quite special, isn't she?" Jondoe says.

"*You're* special!" Shelby cheers, fresh tears springing to her eyes.

"You'll have to forgive us, Melody," Jake says. "We are the proudest parents you are ever likely to meet!"

Proud?

"And we don't get to see too much of our boy these days. Not since he got the call!"

The *call*?

"He has given so much of himself over to his mission." Jake honks into a tissue and tries to get ahold of himself. "Well, we don't have to preach to *you* about the joy of doing the Lord's work. I'm sure your parents are just as proud!"

"I'll tell you *all* about it," Jondoe says to his dad before turning to his mother and asking, "but any chance that a prodigal son can get a home-cooked meal around here first?"

And despite the late hour—it's well past midnight— his mother is all too happy to comply. Of all the grown women and young girls I've watched fall helpless to Jondoe's charms, there is none who is more at his mercy than the one who carried him for nine months in her womb. And his father is equally enthralled by his presence, stopping to turn back and look at him *three times* on the short trip down the hall to the kitchen.

I don't know what to make of all this. There is no way his God-having parents would so happily welcome their son home if they had any idea he was getting rich from premarital sex and sin! If Jondoe is so famous, how has his devilish vocation remained a mystery to his parents? I have to ask.

"Your parents don't know about your . . ." I search for the right word.

"*Job?* Of course they know about my job. That's not a secret. Why do you think they're so happy to see me?"

"They think you're a missionary?" I ask.

"I *am* a missionary." His eyes are twinkling with irrepressible mischief, like one of my housebrothers when he's rigged a bucket of water to fall onto an unsuspecting head. "Surely by now you've guessed my secret?"

I shake my head no, even though I mean yes. I want to hear him say it.

"Gabriel has God too." He taps his fingertip on my nose. "Just." *Tap.* "Like." *Tap.* "You."

This confession should shock me. But it doesn't. And not just because of his parents' showy faithing. His revelation is confirmation of the knowledge I held in my heart all along. Faith is accepting what makes no sense, what we cannot prove, but know down deep in our souls is real.

Now that I've heard it from his lips, that he too has God, everything that has happened to me since leaving Goodside—even my decision *to* leave Goodside—now makes perfect sense of the sort that could never stand up

225

to the scrutiny of the logic and reason revered by Melody and Zen. I know I've done the right thing in leaving Ram behind, even leaving Melody behind, even if my actions have unfortunate unasked-for consequences.

"Come," Jondoe says. "My mom's mac-and-cheese is a taste of Heaven here on earth."

melody

I KNEW ABOUT HARMONY WAY BEFORE SHE KNEW ABOUT ME.

I knew about her because Lib is very good at what he does. The best. So Lib did what any high-stakes broker does: He did a beyond-thorough genetic background check on me, a process made more complicated—and necessary—because of my unknown bioparents.

You know what great lengths I went to to make sure your file was flawless. He'd remind me at least once during every conversation we've ever had. *I put my reputation on the line for you. I pulled strings. I called in favors. I earned my 15 percent.*

I don't know who he paid off or how much he paid out, but Lib gained access to my Good Shepherd Family Placement Services records two years before I was legally allowed to do so myself. And that's how he—we—found out I was, in fact, a monozygotic twin.

At first this was thrilling news. Imagine! A sister! An identical twin! With no genetic connection to my parents, I was fascinated by the possibility of seeing myself in another person. Even though she was a Churchy, I desperately wanted to meet her. There's no closer biological relationship between two people and I just knew that this sister would understand me the way no other person ever had.

"You CANNOT meet her," Lib said. "You CANNOT TELL ANYONE SHE EXISTS."

"Why not?"

"It's very bad for business."

Years later, I'd hear this same line from my parents when they got the news.

"My job is to talk up your unique quotient," Lib explained. "When I make my pitch to affluential parental units, I must convince them that you are the ONLY GIRL ON EARTH whose DNA is designed so deliciously. ONLY YOU can make the DELIVERY of their DREAMS. I can't very well do that if there is someone else who is EXACTLY LIKE YOU and can do the job just as well as you can."

I told him it was unlikely that a Churchy would ever agree to be a Surrogette.

"Helllloooooooo? There are Surrogettes in the Bible," Lib says. "Genesis, chapter sixteen. Sarah gives her maid Hagar to bump with her husband, Abraham."

I had no idea that there was anything in the Bible like that. But I was even more stupidified by the fact that Lib knew so much about it.

"It's my JOB to know things like that, gorgeous. To have the inside angle on any and all competition for my clients. It's what makes me the best." Lib tipped his head back and laughed. "If she was convinced that Surrogetting was a way to serve God, she most certainly would COUNTERFEIT YOU in a THUMPY HEARTBEAT. And because her religion rejects material riches, she'd do it for FREE. Now I ask you: How can YOU compete with THAT? I'll answer: You CAN'T. And that's why SHE is bad for OUR business."

My parents had been prepping me—*pushing* me— toward platinum-level Surrogetting my entire life, even before such arrangements were legal. Ash and Ty predicted that market demands would eventually call for the decriminalization of commercial pregging, and who better than their only daughter to put their theories to the test?

Of course, I didn't think about this when I was fourteen. All I knew then was that I owed my parents for saving me when I was an infant. I couldn't let them down just because the identical twin they *didn't* pick underbid me.

"She isn't your sister," Lib said. "She is the COMPETITION. The ENEMY."

I tried to repeat this out loud to prove how committed I was to our commercial venture. And yet I couldn't bring myself to say the words, to betray this person who was

229

quite possibly my only living blood relative. . . .

"I will never speak of this twin again," Lib said. "And if we are to continue our professional relationship, neither will you."

So I didn't tell my parents—they found out for themselves when Harmony contacted me two years later. I only confided in Zen, who knew this was the one topic for which no questions were allowed. He kept his promise and didn't tell anyone.

Lib, also true to his word, never brought it up again. There was just one hitch: Lib could pay someone off from the Good Shepherd Family Placement Services to expunge Harmony from *my* file, but was powerless to remove me from *hers*.

"It won't matter," he said blithely at the time, the last time we talked about her. "By the time she's old enough to take a looky look, you'll have bumped twice already!"

Well, it didn't quite turn out that way. And now that my secret twin has taken off with my RePro, laying waste to two years of string-pulling and favor-calling and reputation-risking, I'm waiting for Lib's face to combust in a toxic conflagration of synthetic skin.

"So it's your identical *twin*, the Churchy who has God who's bumped pretties with Jondoe."

Ram suddenly comes to.

"Hey, that's my wife you're dishonoring like that!"

The outburst takes me by surprise, and him too, I think. He just as suddenly thuds backward onto the couch

230

as if he's expended his last milligram of energy. Tocin drop.

Lib cackles and claps with delight. "She's *married*?"

"My wife is *not* an adulteress," Ram moans.

Lib is smiling in an unpleasant way. "You all HIGHLY misunderestimate Jondoe's gifts. . . ."

Lib's whatever attitude about this fiasco is giving me a squelchy feeling in my stomach. And it doesn't help that word has gotten out that I'm on the MiVu right now. The screen is filling with 1Vu pop-ups on mute: Celine Lichtblau, Tulie Peters, even Ventura Vida herself mouthing away with her abundant gums. All these bubbleheads think I'm still with Jondoe and hope I'll go into @Vu mode so they can all get a glimpse of the world's hottest RePro for themselves.

"I had NO IDEA I was talking to HER this morning," Lib says.

"You *talked* to her this morning?"

I woke up to what I thought were the sounds of Harmony talking to someone on the MiVu and she denied it. She was on her knees and claimed she was praying. My reproaesthetical ass, she was praying. She was plotting to counterfeit me. Is that really why she came all the way out to Goodside? I assumed that she had wanted to thump me into becoming like her. Is it possible that she really wanted to become more like me?

Lib is still chucking to himself. "It all makes SO MUCH SENSE now. Why she was wearing that TERMINAL nightdress . . . And the freckles!" He leans into the screen to get a closer look at me. "YOU DON'T HAVE FRECKLES AND SHE DOES!" He goes into a whole new fit of giggles.

I'm trembling with fury. And the happier Lib gets, the more off-the-spring crazy I feel. Zen has tightened his grip around my waist, as if to hold me together, to keep me from disintegrating on the spot.

"Where are they now?" Zen asks Lib.

Lib sucks on his polymer veneers.

"WHERE ARE THEY NOW?"

Lib is annoyed that someone as lowly as Zen thinks he can speak to him like that.

"We don't know," he says casually.

"What do you mean you don't know?"

"No one knows. They've gone off grid. I'm SURE they'll turn up after she tests positive."

Holy piss on a stick.

He pauses and quickly shifts to business mode. "So you and . . . what's her name?"

"Harmony," I say.

"Harmony," Lib says, almost as if he's having a private conversation with himself. "She has the same DNA as you? So there's really no difference between you and her? She could be you." Another high-pitched hoot. "Right now she *is* you! Only frecklier!"

It's exactly what Lib had warned me about. We are the same. Interchangeable. Which makes me utterly expendable. And before Lib even gets around to asking if she has representation, I know that he has already given up on me. I am bad business. A worthless investment. But if he plays this right, there's still a chance that he could recoup his losses with the product of Harmony and Jondoe's union. He's already winking and blinking and eye rolling his way to finding my twin before I do. If he has any clue as to where they might be, there's no way he'll let me get to her before he does.

I cannot for another second look at his fake approximation of a face.

"Fuck you, Lib," I say, blinking him out of my view. "And this whole business."

There's a moment of stunned silence before Zen explodes with excitement.

"I always knew you had it in you!"

Zen is still carrying on, clapping and congratulating me for finally standing up for myself, when one of the 1Vu bubbleheads catches my eye. It's Shoko, the only one smart enough to know that I've probably turned off the volume. She's waving a handwritten sign to get my attention. I tap her pop-up to enlarge. It reads:

WATER BROKE! BIRTH CENTER! NOW!

harmony
melody

WE'RE SITTING AROUND THE KITCHEN TABLE, OUR HEADS BENT
over four bowls of orange noodles. My right hand is holding Jondoe's left, my left hand is holding his mother's right,
as his father leads us in prayer.

"Father God, when more than two of us come together
we know that You are with us, and we just come to You
to give up our thanks for all the blessings You have seen fit
to deliver. . . ."

Only my right hand is sweating.

"We just want to thank You, O Lord, for watching over
the hands that made these bowls of macaroni and cheese.
And we also offer our thanks for bringing the beautiful
Melody into our home because her beauty is a gift from
You, O Heavenly Creator. . . ."

Jondoe squeezes my slippery hand.

"And we just want to give our thanks once more for returning our potent son home to us, even if it's just a short while. Because as much as we would like to delight in his company, O Lord, we can't be selfish, we must let him do the work that You have called him to do and we hope that You will continue to protect and bless these two soldiers in Christ's army so they can carry on in their mission to glorify God's kingdom and sow the seeds of faith in His blessed name. Amen."

"Amen," says Shelby.

"A-men to that," says Jondoe.

Everyone's eyes are on me. I am bewildered.

"Amen?"

The prayer finished, the three begin to dig into their bowls.

"Gabriel," his mother says, "please tell us about your mission with Miss Teen Venezuela."

"You read up on that?"

"Oh, Gabey!" his mom says, tousling his hair. "We follow everything you do!"

The tabletop is gray stone tile, and every fourth square is engraved with a different inspirational passage. I look to the wisdom of the Scripture to ground me.

Whether, then, you eat or drink or whatever you do, do all to the glory of God.

I imagine that this is what our kitchen would look like in Goodside if we were allowed to use more than a wood-burning stove, a small propane-fueled refrigerator. My housesisters will be rising with the sun soon enough, gathering wood for the fire in the stove, scrubbing the cows clean for the milking. The Church rejects most modern technologies because an idle life would give us too many free hours to make trouble out of nothing. Melody can't even bring herself to press a button to warm up a meal that was made in a factory on the other side of the world. Too much idle time! It's no wonder her parents try to fill it up for her.

I hope she'll believe me when I say that I never meant to hurt her.

If she ever speaks to me again.

I read another tile.

The soul of the sluggard craves, and gets nothing: but the soul of the diligent is made fat.

Shelby catches me staring.

"You like that verse?" she asks.

"My sisters do," I say. "Work hard at being a good wife and God will reward you with a husband and a big, blessed belly. . . . "

Shelby's eyes light up. I see more of her in Jondoe—and Jondoe in her—when she gets excited.

"How many sisters do you have?"

"Seven."

"Seven!"

Jondoe raises an eyebrow. "Seven?"

"Three have already moved out to start families of

their own," I explain.

"Any brothers?" his mother asks.

"About the same. Six or seven."

The three of them laugh. "You're not sure?" Shelby asks.

Does Ram count as my housebrother now that he's also my husband?

"It's complicated," I say.

"She was adopted," Jondoe explains. "And wants to do for others what her birthmother did for her parental unit. She wants to make a family."

Shelby and Jake have tears in their eyes. "Praise the Lord."

I wonder how many times Jondoe's mother has grown fat from God's rewards.

"Do you have any siblings?" I ask Jondoe.

"You haven't told her about Joshua?" Jake asks.

"No," Jondoe says, examining his reflection in a spoon. He turns it back and forth, concave and convex, his face flipping upside down, right side up, upside down, right side up.

"He's being too modest again," Shelby says in a teasing voice.

"Is Joshua your brother?" I ask.

"Yes," he says. Then he looks away from his own face and says, "He was also my first client."

melody
harmony

GETTING TO THE BIRTH CENTER ISN'T AS EASY AS IT SOUNDS. It's only a few miles away, totally doable by bike, but I need to get myself on the pedal, like, *right now* and Zen is for seriously roadblocking me.

"You can't go alone," he says, placing himself between me and the front door. "You've been through too much already today. . . ."

"You *can't* come with me," I remind him. "You won't be allowed anywhere near the place."

It's totally true. Too many deliveries were getting stolen by black-market traders sneaking into the centers by claiming to be friends and relatives of the birthers. Now access is restricted to a list of vetted guests submitted at least sixty days prior to the due date.

"So what are we supposed to do while you're there?" Zen asks.

A snort rips through the house and shakes the rafters. I refer Zen to the common room, where Ram is in full snore on the couch.

"*You* are going to nanny *him* through his narcoleptic Tocin nap," I say. "Now step aside so I can fulfill my duties as a peer birthcoach."

And Zen does the surprising thing by actually stepping aside the first time I ask. And he continues to do the surprising thing by not saying a word as I unlock my bike. By the time I've turned on all my night-lights, put on my helmet, and am ready to kick off down the gravel, his silence has become more oppressively judgy than anything he could possibly say. I can't take it.

"WHAT?!" I shriek.

He shifts uneasily in his thick-soled sneakers. Five foot seven and a half. Ish. If that.

"I hope it goes better than last time."

I take off toward the birth center without a thank-you or a goodbye.

I put all my energy into pedaling as fast as I can.

Into forgetting about what happened the last time I took this same trip.

I was there when Malia awoke from her Obliterall nap and asked to hold her baby. The nurses told her the delivery had already crossed state lines. She started scream-ing, "Where is my baby? I want my baby! They took my baby!" A half-dozen medical professionals put her in the restraints and gave her enough Obliterall to keep her under for the rest of the day.

I was there eight hours later when she came to. She started right up again with, "Where is my baby? I want my baby! They took my baby!" as if she had never stopped. They knocked her out again.

I was there when she woke up for the third time. She apologized for her hormonal overreaction and convinced everyone that she was back to her nice and normal self. She waited for all the doctors and nurses to leave, looked me dead in the eyes, and said, "*You* let them take my baby." Then she smashed a vase on the floor and slashed both wrists with a jagged triangle of broken glass.

I can't say any more.

Not because I'm not allowed to, but because it hurts too much to remember.

harmony
melody

melody

JONDOE'S FATHER BEGINS THE STORY.

"Joshua is eight years older than Gabriel. He never dated much in high school. In his sophomore year at Somerset Christian College, he fell in love with a sweet girl named Hannah."

"They were both twenty years old," says his mother in a whisper.

I hear the unspoken: God had already closed her womb.

"They got married after graduation . . ."

"It was the most beautiful wedding! What a blessed day!"

"And right away looked into their options for starting a family. They didn't have a lot of money—Joshua works as a youth pastor—not enough to hire professionals anyway.

But Gabey was fourteen at the time, and Hannah's sister, Diana, was sixteen years old and they were both looking to find a way to put their faith into action. . . ."

Jake lets me connect his unfinished sentence to what Shelby says next.

"And now we have one beautiful grandchild with a second on the way!"

Like my housesisters, Jondoe's parents are ignoring the *act*. I guess they'd like to believe that all these births are virgin births, like Mary herself. That is, if it weren't blasphemous to think so. I, however, can't hold my tongue.

"But it's a *sin*!" Then I stop myself because I've forgotten who I'm supposed to be right now. Am I Melody? Or am I me?

Jondoe's parents exchange looks.

"There's nothing wrong with sex," Shelby says. "God invented it, after all. If He didn't want us to do it, He would have designed another way!"

"We're procreationists," Jake tells me.

"Amen to that," Jondoe says.

I'm so confused. The Bible has a *lot* to say on the subject of premarital immorality. Did they somehow miss Paul's letters to the Corinthians?

"But Jondoe and Diana weren't married! Aren't you supposed to believe that bodily sharing is for the marriage bed?"

I say this, but I don't quite believe it myself.

I think about the first—and only—time I lay down

242

with Ram. Or tried to. He was patient and kind and, thinking about the way he shook under the sheets, as petrified as I was. The kiss on the cheek that sealed our marriage was our first brush with intimacy. How could we expose ourselves to each other physically and emotionally just a few hours later? We weren't ready for this—at least not with each other. We put on our clothes, and slept fully dressed and back-to-back until I snuck out.

I never understood how my housesisters were able to give themselves over to their new husbands on their wedding nights.

Then I met Jondoe.

"Sex *is* biblical," Shelby says matter-of-factly. "If you choose to read it that way."

Jondoe is nodding with studied seriousness, the way my housebrothers do during Sunday services when they're only pretending to pay attention.

"The way we see it, Jondoe and Diana were bodily stand-ins for Joshua and Hannah," Jake says. "It was a spiritual marriage, not for pleasure, but for procreation."

Jondoe is biting his lip.

"Look to the Bible," Shelby says.

Here's what I find troublesome about that advice: I know the Bible. Very well. I know it as a curious reader who loves words with little to no access to any other reading material. The Bible contains some of the most inspirational and miraculous stories ever put to paper, but also some of the most vicious and vile acts imaginable. Mass murder!

Human sacrifice! Inappropriate affections with livestock! I know the verses that the preachers don't like to talk about on Sundays. I also know that you can find a verse to support just about any argument, and another verse to shut it down. If it's all the Word of God, how can we simply ignore the parts that don't fit our beliefs?

I was twelve when I asked Ma these questions; she said, "You better not let your husband hear you ask questions like that."

I was told to put my faith in the Council, who knew more about the Scriptures than I did. They would tell me what verses to read. And they would tell me what to think.

And now, four years later, I don't know what to think about anything.

Which, as I'm finally realizing, is exactly the way the Church wants it.

Jondoe clears his throat. All eyes are on him.

"Humans are sexual beings," Jondoe says. "Instead of fighting our natural, God-given urges, we should find the best way to use them to glorify His kingdom."

When he speaks, it's like I can't *not* listen. And believe.

"I've got this great gift," Jondoe says, speaking for himself for the first time. "A gift that can really help people and bring them happiness and fulfillment in their lives. I'm giving people what they want more than anything else on this earth, but can't get without my help." His eyes are brighter, his face flushed. "You know, before the Virus, people created life in a petri dish. No intimacy! I think it's deep that two souls come together as one body and create a new life."

A one-flesh union, I think to myself.

"To me, it's even deeper when *four* souls come together and create a new life."

When he puts it like that, it does sound divine.

"Our granddaughter, Ruthie, is truly the most precious angel that you will ever lay eyes on," Shelby says.

She shows me a picture of a cherubic toddler who looks like a tiny version of . . . herself! It's no wonder that she's so taken with her granddaughter. This is a possibility I had never considered before: I might see my unknown birthmother's face reflected in that of my own child.

"Ruthie has brought so much joy into all our lives," Shelby says, before turning to Jondoe. "*You* have brought so much joy into our lives and the lives of so many others!"

Jondoe lowers his head, closes his eyes. A humbled pose.

"He got the call," Jake says, clapping his son on the shoulder. "To do the Lord's work in his own unique way."

"Not everyone gets the call," Shelby says wistfully. "But my son did and answered it!"

Jondoe pushes his bowl away and stands up.

"Speaking of," he says. "It's about time we got down to ministrations."

His parents hold out their hands for us to take.

"'Behold, children are a heritage from the LORD, the fruit of the womb a reward,'" Jake prays. "'Like arrows in the hand of a warrior are the children of one's youth. How blessed is the man whose quiver is full of them! He shall not be ashamed.' Amen."

His parents look at me eagerly, hoping that I'll be able identify the verse. But I don't. I can't. I'm speechless.

His parents know exactly why I'm here and what Jondoe's intentions are.

And they couldn't be happier about it.

melody
harmony

A LARGE SIGN AT THE ENTRANCE TO IVY OBSTETRICS AND Birthing Center reads:

NO INFANTS ON PREMISES
All deliveries are brought to separate processing
facilities immediately following postpartum approval
screenings by the Newborn Quality Testing Service

I reluctantly approach the security kiosk.

"I'm here for Shoko Weiss."

The guard slouches over her screen and starts finger-swiping. Like many obsolescents, she's obliterated any signs of her ancestry with a total body overhaul. This is fresh work. Everything from the slant of her green eyes and the delicate slope of her nose to her toasty brown skin and white-blond Afro is all right on trend for the season. She could be from all continents, or none at all. She could be from another galaxy.

"Name?" she asks, without looking at me.

"Melody Mayflower."

Her head jolts up.

"Melody Mayflower?" Her squinty eyes are bulging beyond capacity. "Omigod."

Uh-oh. I was afraid of this. That they would remember me from last time. That I was the one with the girl who went all Postpartum Psychotic on them. They don't want to take any chances this time around.

The guard is fumbling with the pen. "Um, could you sign this?"

I do.

With a shaking hand, she taps to clear the screen.

"Can you? I mean, do you think you could? Would it be possible for you to . . . ?" She holds out the pen once more.

I don't remember having to sign in more than once last time, but I'm not going to argue unnecessarily.

She taps a few more times.

"And just one more time?" she asks. "Only this time, write something like, 'To Poe: Be breedy! Love, Melody Mayflower.'"

I drop the pen. "WHAT?"

"It's for my little sister," she explains. "She's, like, your biggest fan."

I have *fans*?

I sign the autograph anyway because it seems easier than *not* signing the autograph and having this girl put out on the MiNet that I'm a for seriously starcissistic bitch who won't sign autographs.

I race right up to the front doors, not even bothering to lock my bike before ditching it in the bushes and rushing through to the second security checkpoint. When I get there, I'm greeted by a second guard who must have gone to the same surgeon because she looks almost identical to the first.

She too has a pen in hand.

Before I can ask to whom I should sign the autograph, my hand is seized by one of the wrinkliest ladies I've seen in a long time. For serious, she's old enough to have biological children *and* grandchildren. I know she works here because she's wearing the scrubs worn by all staff members: pink and blue stripes entwined with embroidered ivy leaves.

"I'm Madison Lutz-Lewis! Branch manager!"

She's got a shockingly firm grip.

"I'm Melody May—"

"I know who you are! *Everyone* knows who you are!" I try to shake her off, but she will not let go of my hand. "We're beyond excited to host a celebrity! We're aware that you could choose to deliver anywhere in the world, but we do hope that when it's your time to deliver your precious pregg, you will at least consider Ivy Obstetrics and Birthing Center."

I pry her mottled claw from my flesh. "I'm not here for a tour. I'm here to help my friend."

"Yes!" she yips. "Miss Weiss!"

Ms. Lutz-Lewis has only one mode: POSITIVE! But it's a relief to talk to someone who seems like she might know something worth knowing.

"You can't see her!"

"I can't? Why not?" I'm about to go diva on her ass. If I'm such a celebrity, I might as well start abusing all the privileges that come with it.

"Miss Weiss is in the OR."

"The OR? So she's having a cesarean?"

Part of me actually smiles at this, thinking it's *so* Shoko to get exactly what she wanted with this second pregg. She swore after the first one turned her breedy bits into a U.S. Buff-A burger (her words) that she was going to let them go in through the belly the second time around.

"No more pushing," she had insisted. "This time they can pull the sucker out."

"I can't comment on births in progress." Ms. Lutz-Lewis is still smiling, but the tiniest deflation in tone tells me that Shoko is not having a routine C-section.

"Please," I whisper. "She's my best friend."

Ms. Lutz-Lewis puts her hand on my back and gives a gentle push.

"Take a seat in our waiting area and one of our highly trained medical professionals will come talk to you shortly. In the meantime we will do everything we can to accommodate your every need! We have fresh linens for guests pulling all-nighters."

It's way past midnight and I'm too exhausted to argue anyway. I trudge to the waiting room, which is also decorated in the infantile pastels and twining ivy motif. The room is empty except for a brittle blond piece of plastic I instantly recognize as Destinee, Shoko's RePro Rep. She's a ruthless cradlegrabber who used to work in corporate real estate before shifting her focus to human property. I know her well because she has repeatedly tried to woo me away from Lib.

"I recall that your last experience at our center was not optimal. . . ." Ms. Lutz-Lewis is in full pitch mode. "And I hope that we can prove to you that we may not be the fanciest, but we do run a top-notch facility."

I ditch Ms. Lutz-Lewis to interrupt Destinee's MiChat. "Destinee!" I cry out. "What's happening to Shoko?"

Destinee pretends she's thrilled to see me and apologizes to whomever she's speaking to.

"The delivery is one hundred percent perfect," Destinee says to me in a voice as tight as her face.

"That's not what I asked!" I say. "How is Shoko?"

Every time I say Shoko's name, Destinee twitches inside her shimmery suit. This only makes me want to push more.

"WHERE IS SHOKO? I NEED TO SEE SHOKO."

"Let's finish this conversation in facespace tomorrow when you pick up your delivery," she MiChats. "Congratulations, again!"

Then she blinks off, rips out her earbud, and collapses into a chair right next to latest ad from the Save America Society. It presents real girls and their awesome thoughts on pregging. Every five seconds, a new girl. A new reason to pregg.

PREGGING IS . . . PRETTY!

"I was MiChatting with Shoko's *investors*, the Ruiz-Lees," she says. "And they're already worried about their delivery and don't need you getting all shouty in the background."

PREGGING IS . . . PROUD!

"*What* happened? What's going on?"

Destinee takes a pack of smokeless cigs out of her bag, removes one from the box, and takes a long, hard pull before answering.

PREGGING IS . . . POWERFUL!

"The delivery is one hundred percent perfect," she repeats. And before I can remind her that she's said this already, she adds, "But it will be the last one Shoko ever makes."

harmony
melody

WE STAND IN FRONT OF A CLOSED DOOR ON THE SECOND
floor. I don't wait for him to invite me in before opening
it myself.

I'm initiating.

And I like it.

"This is my room," Jondoe says. "Or *was*."

The room comes as bit of a surprise.

"My parents have kept it just as I left it," he explains.
"They don't seem to realize that I'm not fourteen years old
anymore. I'm not the same person I was when I left."

This room certainly does not look like it was ever
inhabited by a world-famous sophisticate. It's more like
a child's playroom, with half the space taken up by a
messy assemblage of knee pads, shin guards, and helmets,

surfboards, snowboards, and other sporting equipment I don't recognize.

"Go ahead," he says softly. "Take a look around."

One wall collage is covered in images of a younger Jondoe flipping in midair and otherwise defying gravity with or without one of his boards.

A second wall collage brings him closer to earth. He's licking a vanilla ice-cream cone, holding a trophy over his head, getting hugged by his parents.

It's the third wall that really gets my attention. There's a line drawing of Christ riding on a skateboard. Underneath the words:

SERVE THE LORD ON THE BOARD

X–TREME YOUTH MINISTRIES

"That was my passion," Jondoe says, his voice right in my ear. "Before I found my true calling."

He places his hand on the small of my back. I know I should inch away but it feels like his hand should have been there all along.

"Don't you think it's disrespectful to show our Savior in that way?"

"Jesus was as extreme as it gets!" exclaims Jondoe. "I mean, think of all the cool shit He does in the New Testament. He rocks all those miracles and then He goes out of His way to be a friend to all, the freaks and whores, everyone. He's got major rebel cred, right? That's how I see myself."

His hand moves in a slow circular motion.

"But Jesus never tried to deny who He was," I reply. "How are you serving Him through your work if no one knows the truth about you?"

A warmth spreads across my lower back, around, and down.

"My partners see the Truth with a capital *T*," Jondoe says. "Maybe not before or after, but definitely *during*."

I'm afraid to ask what he means by this.

"I make them see God. Or rather, God, working through me, helps them see God. He gets all the credit. Only our Creator has the power to stir such feelings of ecstasy. Each and every one of my preggs has been touched by His divine hand."

His hand . . .

His hand is under my shirt!

"The more I give to God, the more blessings I'll receive in return," he whispers into my ear. "I'll never be able to outgive Him, but I'm having fun trying."

His hand is not one or two—it feels like thousands of hands roaming all over my body, even in the hidden places he hasn't dared to touch. He is leaning into me and I feel as if I'm hyptonized. I should move away, I should . . .

"Oh!"

He's pressing his mouth against mine.

I'm receiving him and he's receiving me.

I'm losing myself and finding myself.

Through the sublime transcendence of this kiss.

melody
harmony

POSTPARTUM HEMORRHAGING IS SOMETHING WE LEARN ABOUT in birthing class. Not even a whole class. Half a class— fifteen minutes—devoted to "Bad Things That Could Happen But Totally Won't So Don't Worry About It." We're told that teenage girls just like us have been the most prolific breeders throughout human history and advances in modern medicine have eliminated nearly all the risks. "Placenta accreta," "preeclampsia," "uterine atony," "hypovolemic shock," "diminished myometrial contrac- tability" are nothing more than multiple-choice responses on a exam. "Postpartum psychosis" is also something that we learned about. It too had (A), (B), (C), (D) answers to choose from, but never happens in real life. Or if it does, not to anyone we actually know.

So we are told.

Shoko nearly bled to death when her uterus failed to contract after it afterbirthed. And she might have too, if the on-site surgeon hadn't rushed her into the OR and removed her uterus with a million-dollar laser.

I cannot believe this is happening. First Malia. Now Shoko. Who's next?

"She's recovering fine now," Destinee insists in between drags. "But this is definitely a deal breaker for pregg number three."

I want to strangle this horrible woman with her hair extensions but she's my only source of information.

"Where are Shoko's parents?" I ask. "Raimundo?"

A lung-rattling sigh. "They annoyed her too much last time, so she didn't put them on the guest list for delivery this time. They'll probably stop by tomorrow."

"So we're the only ones here for Shoko?" I'm afraid to hear the truth.

"You are," she says pointedly. "Because I'm beyond tired and need to get some sleep before I face the Ruiz-Lees tomorrow and have to explain why a hysterectomy is not a violation of their option agreement."

She click-clacks toward the exit but stops before going through it.

"And by the way," she says with acid condescension. "If *I* were your Rep, *I* would've sealed the deal with Jon-doe two years ago."

I'm beyond terminated at this point. Even if I had the

energy to make the ride home, I wouldn't.

I take a pillow and blanket left behind by Ms. Lutz-Lewis and curl into the couch, committed to staying the night. Someone needs to be here for Shoko when she wakes up. As her birthcoach, that's the very least I can do. But this time, I won't just be there, I'll be there for *her*.

More than I was for Malia.

harmony
melody

I AWAKE NOT IN PANIC, NOR IN PRAYER.

At peace.

Jondoe is still sleeping beside me, warm and sweet.

I arose to open for my lover

I am my lover's

And my lover is mine. . . .

It wasn't a dream.

We are still naked.

I am still unashamed.

Eyes still closed, Jondoe nuzzles his beard into my bare shoulder.

"Melody," he says. "Now, *that* was something."

He knew me last night. But he still doesn't *know* me.

Before this goes any further, I have to tell the truth. Not because the Church has taught me that to do otherwise is a sin, but because I know I must.

"I have a confession to make. And after I make it, I will understand if you hate me."

"I already know that I could never hate anyone who is capable of making me feel the way I'm feeling right now."

His is the kindest, gentlest voice I've ever heard.

"You might."

"I promise you," he says, "I won't."

I take a deep breath to brace myself. When I exhale, the words come out all in a rush. "Because I'm not who you think I am. I'm not the girl in the file."

My chest tightens, my throat clamps shut, and my eyes fill with tears. And before I can explain further, a look of relief falls over Jondoe's beautiful face. He takes my hands in his, squeezes them gently.

"And I'm not the man in my file either!" Jondoe replies cheerfully. "We know this already."

I'm ready to give my confession, but Jondoe isn't willing to receive it. I try again.

"What I mean is, I'm not Melody. I'm not the girl you're being paid to . . ." I can't say it.

"Shhhhhhhh," he says, pressing a finger to his own lips, which only makes me wish he were pressing it against mine. "Let's not talk business right now."

He rolls on top of me and—oh my grace—there it is again!

"Not when there's still time for pleasure."

The bone of his bones . . . The flesh of his flesh . . .

"I have a twin!" I cry out.

melody
harmony

I'M YANKED OUT OF SLEEP BUT NOT QUITE INTO FULL
consciousness. My eyeballs are vibrating and my ears are
crackling. Someone has a hand on my shoulder.

"Are you okay?" a voice asks.

No, I'm not okay. I'm for seriously janked. I blindly
grab around inside my shoulder bag to find the carrying
case for my MiNet contacts and earbuds. I always have
the mindhumpiest dreams when I forget to remove them
before I fall asleep.

Ventura Vida was the first Southeast Asian–American
woman president of the United States. She was giving a
speech.

"Only you can choose how and when you want to
pregg. The power is yours!"

And then I charged the stage.

"Power? We don't have any power! Not until we can make the choice to have un-preggy sex!"

And President Vida was all like, "There's a delivery deficit of epic proportions! You have the rest of your life to hump around!"

And I didn't get the chance for a comeback because that's when I woke up. I must have been picking up on someone's MiNet newsfeed or something. But, whoa, it felt more real than any 4-D role-play at the Avatarcade.

I rub out my MiNet contacts, pry away my earbuds, and put them away. It takes a few seconds to adjust to reality.

"I'm Freya," chirps the pigtailed pre-pubie whose hand still rests on my shoulder.

She's looks even younger than the girls I saw in Babiez R U over the weekend. She's wearing one of those horrible "Born to Breed" Ts that must be so on trend at the elementary school right now, only the lettering on her shirt is nearly stretched beyond legibility because she was talked into buying a FunBump way too big for her tiny frame. She looks like she could topple over and faceplant any second now.

I push myself up into a sitting position, still trying to reorient myself to my surroundings. It's a little after nine a.m. No wonder my whole body hurts. I slept in a twisted ball on this uncompromising couch for six hours.

Freya is still standing there, staring at me with these

huge anime eyes. Without saying anything, she hands me a cold can of Coke '99 and a Chocolate Chip Glyco-GoGo Bar. It's my favorite flavor and I don't hesitate to tear open the wrapper. Oh, sweet chemical fortification! I pop open the can and take a big swig of soda. I can feel myself returning to this waking world as the vitamins and minerals do their job.

This pre-pubie is obviously obsessed with pregging because she's gawking at my flat tummy as if it's the most unlookawayable site she's ever seen. I know she's young, but she's old enough to know that such blatant bumpwatching is just about the rudest thing you can do to someone in my concave condition.

"Thanks," I say, holding up the remainder of the bar and soda.

"Your favorite flavors? Right?" She claps her hands eagerly. "Right?"

"Ummmm, right."

And just as it strikes me as odd for this girl to have any knowledge of my favorite snack foods, she rushes forward to press her palms to my navel.

"Hey!" I scold, gently slapping her away. "Hands off!"

"Sorry!" she says, sounding more apoplectic than apologetic. "I just can't believe I'm this close to *Jondoe's pregg*!"

I poke a finger in my empty ear, just to make sure I'm not having another aural hallucination.

"What's Jondoe *really* like?"

Just hump me now. How could I have forgotten that

my most bizarre nightmare is still a reality?

"Good morning!"

It's Ms. Lutz-Lewis, relentlessly chipper for a grammy who was up as late as I was. Did she even go home last night? Does she live here? I'm about to ask when I remember something important: I don't give a damn.

"Pleeeeeeease! Just tell me!" The arrival of Ms. Lutz-Lewis has made Freya more desperate for answers. "Is Jondoe *really* erection perfection like it says on the MiNet?" She for seriously looks like she's going to pee herself.

I open my mouth to tell her that she's too young to be asking such pervy questions when Ms. Lutz-Lewis for seriously loses it.

"MISS FREYA ALEXANDER. What are you doing out of your room?"

"I got bored."

"You're not here to make friends!" She swoops in on the little girl. "You're here to make a delivery!"

Waaaait. That's *not* a FunBump she's wearing? Freya is not a day older than eleven. Has she even lost all her first teeth? She can't fill a training bra! And anyone with eyes can see that she doesn't have adequate hip width. There's no way she's pushing it out. They'll have to cut and pull.

"Wah," whines the girl, acting every bit the kid she is.

Ms. Lutz-Lewis has her by a bony elbow and tries to guide her back to her room.

"When's this thing gonna be borned?" Freya hollers. "Borning is soooooo boring!"

"Now, now. With an attitude like that, you'll *never* win the FedEx 'We Live to Deliver' Scholarship. . . . "

GAAAAAH! She hasn't graduated from elementary school yet! She shouldn't be worrying about college scholarships! Especially one that requires her to pregg every calendar year between now and obsolescence! I don't even need to ask who put her up to it because I know the answer all too well: her parents.

There are reasons why commercial pregging is illegal under the age of thirteen. Who *did* this girl bump with? Her *boyfriend*? I've read about so-called preemie pregging in the third world, but it's not something you see in suburbs like Princeton, where it's a very, *very* down-market thing to do.

As it was once down-market at my school for anyone at any age to pregg for profit.

Until I signed on with Lib.

And everyone tried to follow. And if they couldn't get a deal like mine, they hoped to go from amateur to pro. Just like Shoko.

Is Freya the future? Will there be a time where there will be no such thing as too young to pregg? Zen swears that the Chinese are plumping their newborns with the same hypergrowth hormones that can turn an egg into a bucket of fried chicken in fourteen days (growth hormones being a subject of great interest to him, for obvious reasons).

"I'm so bored," the girl whines. "And my tummy hurts."

I'm sick to my stomach. And it's not sympathetic labor pains.

"Oh! In all this commotion I nearly forgot to tell you!" Ms. Lutz-Lewis calls out. "Miss Weiss is ready for visitors now!"

I'm not ready for her.

harmony
melody

"A TWIN."

Jondoe laughs uneasily, searching my face to find a trace of humor or anything else that will explain why I just said what I said.

"*She's* Melody and—"

He puts a finger to my lips to hush me up.

"Shhhh. We are so alike. It's like you're the girl version of me."

"I am?"

"I'm vibing on everything you're saying right now," he says. "I've spent a lot of time on the therapist's couch, so I get it, the whole twin thing. You woke up this morning feeling guilty about everything we did last night."

An angelic smile takes wing across his lips.

"Actually, I don't feel guil—"

He keeps talking. "You created a twin self to represent the contradictory parts of your psyche, your soul—"

"What?" I honestly have no idea what he's talking about. By the unguarded look in his eyes, I know he is thoroughly convinced that what he is saying is the irrefutable truth.

"You have trouble reconciling the dual parts of your personality." He brushes his lips against my neck. "The part that wants to be prayerful and pure, and the other part that wants to experience more . . ." He nibbles on my earlobe. "Earthly delights."

I push him off me. "Nonononono," I protest, flaming from the inside out. "I'm *really* Melody's twin."

His eyes light up. He smiles more broadly than ever before.

"Oooh, you *are* a fun one. You're taking it to a whole new level!" He looks at me with admiration. "You're even more complex than I could have ever imagined. More than any girl I've been paired with before."

"Really?"

"Um-hm." He dances a fingertip across my lips, down my chin, and across my collarbone. "You're my perfect match."

"But you don't even know who I am! My real name is Harmony."

Jondoe doesn't react with anything resembling surprise. He seems completely unfazed by this revelation.

"You can be whoever you want to be."

"I barely know *who* I am! I'm not ready for all of this!"

Jondoe attempts a serious face, but he's still grinning in his eyes.

"God will never tempt you with more than you can withstand. . . ."

I groan. "I don't need Corinthians right now."

"Okay, then. How about this?" Jondoe pauses. "Nothing about you is a surprise to God. He knew I would become part of you. Your life."

"Speak from your own heart!"

"I'm sorry," he says. "I'm kinda off script right now."

"Off Scripture?"

"No," he says. "Off *script*. I mean, just when I get into the whole godfreaky thing, you want to change it up on me again with this twin thing."

I bristle at the word "godfreaky." Why would he put it that way? Maybe the word isn't as harsh or hateful out here as it is where I come from. . . .

"I like Harmony," he says.

"You do?"

"I do," he says decisively.

"And it really doesn't matter that I'm not Melody?"

Jondoe kisses the freckles on my nose.

"I promise this is just the beginning for you and me. But right now, we must complete our mission," he says, rolling back on top of me. "So let's assume the position. . . ."

melody
harmony

I DON'T KNOW WHAT I'M EXPECTING TO SEE WHEN I GET TO Shoko's room. But I certainly don't expect to find her healthy enough to be sitting upright in her bed wolfing down on a double U.S. Buff-A burger and grooving along to Fed Double X on MiTunes.

"Ima bump-bump-da-bump-da-bump-bump N grind. Gots 2 hump-hump-da-hump-da-hump-hump U so fine. . . ."

"Hey Shoko," I say tentatively. "I'm so sorry—"

"M-M-M-Mel!" mumbles Shoko between mouthfuls of meat. "You *should* be sorry!" She sets down her burger on the tray, wipes the ketchup off her hands with a paper napkin, then huffily folds her arms across her chest.

When they drop awkwardly into her lap she looks down and laughs. "Oops. I forgot I don't have my built-in belly shelf anymore."

"I'm really sorry, Shoko," I say quickly. "I'm sorry I wasn't here in time to coach you through the delivery."

"You're sorry about *that*?" She looks genuinely surprised. "Oh, don't be sorry about that. There was no way I could hold in the Burrito until you got here. The nurse says they had just enough time to hit me with Obliterall before it just kinda shot out!" She thwacks her palm over her open mouth. *POP!*

"So what am I sorry for?"

"For not telling your *best friend* that you're bumping with Jondoe! I mean, we were just talking about him yesterday! I don't know whether I should scream *at* you or squee *with* you!"

I press my face into my hands. Where do I even go with this?

"TELL ME EVERYTHING," Shoko demands, bouncing up and down in her bed. "Is Jondoe as reproaesthetical in person as he is in 4-D?"

"Um . . . about that," I say, taking a deep breath.

"Does he smell like a heady and penetrating combination of cinnamon, black pepper, amber, and tobacco?"

"What?"

"Does he smell like Jondoe: the Fragrance?"

"I don't know," I say, trying to hide my irritation. "Because it wasn't me with him last night. I've got an identical twin sister."

And before I lose my nerve, I go on to tell her the whole crazy story.

That my twin's name is Harmony and we were separated at birth and she grew up in a Churchy settlement with the thumpiest trubies and she showed up in my face-space for the very first time two? three? whatever days ago and *she's* the one who was with Jondoe last night, not me, *she's* the one who has probably bumped with him by now, not me, because I've never met him and so I have no idea if he smells like cinnamon or recycled grease or what.

Shoko stabs a fry into a bloody splurt of ketchup. She says nothing.

"You don't believe me, do you?"

And why should she? I don't believe it and it's happening to me.

"If you have a special confidentiality clause in your contract," Shoko says darkly, "you could have just said so. You didn't have to make up some bullshitty story."

She stuffs the uneaten half of her hamburger into the crinkly plastic bag and pushes away the tray.

It's pointless to tell the truth. I could present a 4-D of my unbroken hymen and Shoko would still insist that the ability to pregg without full penetration is proof of Jondoe's unrivaled artistry and expertise. Until Shoko sees me standing side by side with my identical twin in her face-space, she's never going to believe that Harmony isn't me.

"I'm sorry, Shoko, you know how these deals are," I

say cagily. "But I promise to tell you everything as soon as I'm allowed to."

She leans forward in the bed. "Just tell me." She raises a very serious eyebrow. "Cinnamon?"

I nod because why the hell not? Shoko swoons. But if she starts asking if Jondoe sounds like sunshine and tastes like sprinkle-dipped rainbows, I'm done.

"Oooh! It's nine thirty! Time for more Humerall!"

Humerall, the less amorous pharmacological cousin to Tocin. She presses a button at her bedside and within seconds I can see all tension release itself from her face and shoulders. She oozes into her pillows, her eyes soft and her lips spread into a dreamy smile.

"Cinnamon . . . cinnamon . . . cinnamon," she mutters happily to herself. Then she snaps into focus. "We should make a cinnamon-flavored snack fortified with Tocin. And you know what we should call it?"

I hazard a guess. "Tocinnamon somethings?"

"YES!" she says, slapping the mattress. "Tocinnamon somethings. We should for seriously invent that."

If Shoko was ragey a minute ago, she isn't now.

"Sooooooo . . ." I venture. "Do you remember anything about your delivery?"

She gives me the side eye. "Ummmmm, hello? Obliterall!"

"Um." I broach the subject as gently as possible. "You almost, like, *died*, Shoko. Did anyone mention that?"

"Sorta," she says, her head slithering like an intoxicated snake. "I got all bleedy or whatever and they had to suck

274

out most of my breedy bits." She makes a nauseating slurpy sound and twists into the pillows in a fit of giggles. "So no more preggs for me." Her face clouds for a moment. "You know what makes me sad?"

"That you almost died?"

She ignores me. "I have to wait eight weeks to recover from my hystericalectomy,"

"Hysterectomy."

"Whatever," she says. "I'll have to wear a one-piece all summer. Because by the time I get my tummy trim, swimsuit season will be over!"

I can't believe this conversation.

"You almost died."

"But I didn't," she says, grinning. "I'm still here. And I don't remember a thing."

"I know you don't remember, which is why I'm reminding you."

"If you don't stop being so dramatic, I'm gonna have to ask the nurse to give me more Humerall."

And then she turns up the music.

"Investin' like da stock mockey
Get yoself a cock jockey
Partyin' at MasSEX
Deliverin' Fed Double X. . . ."

Shoko's blankets pop up and down with every attempt at a hip thrust.

275

"I don't think grinding is a good idea right now," I say. "Um, considering you almost died yesterday."

Shoko sucks in her cheeks. "Oy vey. I am for seriously regretting approving you for my guest list. You are being so neggy right now."

I sit down beside her. Time to get tough. "Shoko. You're my best friend and you almost died. And for what?"

She looks stunned. "For *what*? Are you listening?"

"No."

She rewinds the music, turns it up, then raps along:

"Take yo pillz 2 get no illz
Bump yo skillz 2 pay da billz. . . ."

Gaaaaah. I have to say it: If I could abort Fed Double X, I would.

"So 'for what?'" Shoko repeats. "For my *future*. So I can pay for a decent college without having to take out a quarter-million dollars in loans. So I can get a decent job and make decent money. So when I'm old I can afford to pay a high school girl like me to push out a pregg of my own someday."

She's totally overlooking that she just pushed out a pregg of her own and gave it away to a couple she's never met without even looking at him. Or her. Or whatever it was. I can't blame her for thinking this way. Because until very recently, I had bought into it all too.

"Don't get all judgy, Mel," she says. "Just because I

haven't bumped with a billion-dollar spermbank doesn't make me, you know, down-market."

That is a misconception in every sense of the word. I attempt the truth once more.

"But I haven't bumped with Jondoe!"

"Remind me to resume this conversation with you whenever that confidentiality clause runs out." With that, she rings the nurse for more Humerall.

I take that as a sign to make my exit from Ivy Obstetrics and Birthing Center. Unfortunately, Ms. Lutz-Lewis won't let me go quietly.

"I've taken the liberty of MiNetting you the most up-to-the-moment information about our staff and services!" she exclamates. "We hope you'll think local when choosing your birth facility."

With those words, it hits me. I know exactly what to do to put an end to this crazy charade.

"Oh," I say casually, "I won't be needing your birthing services."

Every wrinkle droops with disappointment.

"Don't take it personally," I say. "It's just that I won't be needing *any* birthing services. From anyone."

Ms. Lutz-Lewis is confounded. "But . . . you . . . and Jondoe . . ."

We have gathered a little crowd of winking blinking onlookers. Freya, of course, and several others, even Shoko has gotten out of bed to gawk. Great. The more MiNet footage, the better.

"Jondoe and I had un-preggy sex!" I declare, getting flushed just by the thought of it. "For pleasure. Because we are in looooooooove."

"What?!" The whole group is scandalized, but none more than Ms. Lutz-Lewis. "Making love? At *your* age?"

"Yes!" I say proudly, making deliberate eye contact with every set of eyes. "With CONDOMS!"

If that sound bite doesn't coax Jondoe and Harmony out of hiding for a damage-control rebuttal, nothing will.

The devastating impact of this word is stunning and immediate. Ms. Lutz-Lewis looks like she's about to faint into the arms of a nervous nurse. Freya and the rest of the girls don't see her, don't see me, don't see anything at all except the MiNet and who can be the first to launch this footage and exploit its famegaming potential.

Only Shoko is nervy enough to address me directly.

"You were telling the truth before, weren't you?" she whispers. "About the twin?"

"Yes," I say quickly. "Why do you believe me now?"

"Because even *that* makes more sense than *this*."

Ms. Lutz-Lewis is muttering something about condoms, starting to come to her senses.

"You better get out of here before they diagnose you with *pre*-partum psychosis," Shoko urges.

She's right. I've got no time to waste. There's no way I can go home. By the time I get there, it'll be surging with paps hoping to catch me screaming about rubbers . . . if they aren't already.

I message Zen.

911. GET OUT.

Two seconds later, he responds.

OK. OUR SPOT?

Not even a second passes after I say YES before Zen has the same response as a billion other MiNet commenters following Jondoe and Melody Mayflower's newsfeed.

CONDOMS?!??!

harmony

melody

MY SECOND AWAKENING IS SO MUCH WORSE THAN THE FIRST.

I'm alone.

The sheets are damp and clammy against my bare skin.

And I hear voices raised in anger right below me.

"PLEASE tell me that you were SCAMMING."

I recognize the voice from the MiVu. It's Lib. And he does not sound happy.

"Now you're some kind of GODFREAK."

That word again. I shiver.

"Dose down," I hear Jondoe say. "I did what I had to do to get the job done. . . ."

"What EXACTLY were you THINKING bringing HER here?!"

Guilt drops a stone in my gut. I know that I'm the

HER. This argument is about me.

And what I've done.

"You're not even my agent—why do you care about my business?" Jondoe is asking. "Anyway, all traces of Gabriel have been trashed from my file. . . ."

I hear cruel laughter. "Your business is Melody's business and her business is my business. It's my JOB to rewrite files like yours. To keep all those dirty little secrets *secret*. I'm the one who found out that my client even *had* a twin. . . ."

"Are you *sure* I've got the wrong one upstairs?"

Wrong one? If I'm the wrong one, does that make Melody the right one?

Lib cackles again. "You didn't think it was at all weird when she started calling herself by a different name and got all THUMPY on you?"

I told him I wasn't Melody!

"I thought that was her *avatar*," Jondoe says.

He didn't believe me.

"Her AVATAR? We're not playing GAMES here, Jondoe."

He thought I was Melody the entire time . . . ?

"A lot of these Surrogettes are into the whole 4-D role-playing thing. It's a technique their positive energists recommend to help distance themselves from the whole experience, another layer of detachment between the Surrogette and the delivery. So it's, like, you know, another coping mechanism."

The love he gave wasn't meant for me, but for my sister?

"Myyyyyy. SUCH BIG WORDS YOU HAVE. SOMEONE has spent a lot of time getting SHRINKY."

"I was just playing along. I spent the first fourteen years of my life pretending to be as perfect as my brother. I figured a few hours wouldn't be a problem."

Wait . . . Jondoe doesn't have God?

And Gabriel *never* did?

Why would he lie?

"I just wanted to get down to business. But then—"

"Did you?" Lib interrupts.

"What kind of limpdick do you take me for?" Jondoe asks, anger rising in his voice. "You think I don't know when I've hit my target?"

Lib laughs. It's a hard, hateful sound and it makes me physically ill. Sickness comes on like a stampede inside my stomach. I have just enough time to grab one of Jondoe's helmets into which I spew the toxic contents of my gut.

"Her egg was blasted by the fastest sperm ever recorded! Of COURSE you did your job."

I'm gasping for air, grasping the ugly truth.

Jondoe doesn't love God.

He doesn't love me.

I was just another job.

This insight brings on a second wave of violent nausea. But this time nothing comes up. There's nothing left.

I've never felt so used up in my entire life.

"The deal is done," Jondoe says in a low growl. "Anything less would do major damage to my brand at this phase of my career."

"But you should make her piss on a stick just to be sure it's in there."

It's in there.

In *where*? In here?

I knock on my emptied belly as if expecting a tiny fist to knock back from the inside.

In *here*.

Do I feel any different?

No.

And yet . . .

I know in my soul that Jondoe is right.

A life is starting inside me.

melody
harmony

I'M WAITING FOR ZEN IN OUR SPOT. THE TREE HOUSE.

The tree house isn't a real tree house. It's a plastic tree house in the children's library on the University campus. It's a library as in ink-on-paper books with *pages*, so the whole place kind of smells weird, like mildew and rotting logs. Needless to say it's beyond boring and retro and there are never any kids here. Every few years someone petitions the University in the attempt to demo the whole place and build a Kiddie Avatarcade or something in its place, but it's protected by some historic preservation act through the next decade.

One of my many babysitters or nannies or tutors loved every MiNet-blinded inch of the place. He or she—I can't remember, there were so many of these educators and caregivers over the years—brought me here all the time when I was little, even after he or she discovered the hard way that I'm for seriously allergic to ink on paper. I might get a little sniffly and sneezy, but I won't have a massive allergic reaction as long as I don't attempt to turn any pages. Just cracking the binding of *The Cat in the Hat* almost put me in anaphylactic shock when I was three.

Despite the risks—or perhaps because of them—the tree house became my go-to for secret-giving-and-taking. It's the only place in town we could guarantee we wouldn't be watched by electronic or fleshy eyeballs. The tree house, in fact, is where Zen wrote and I signed the secret pact four years ago.

His face is sticking out the plastic window when I arrive.

"We could have met at the house because most of the paps already left," he says. "You're only trending in the top twenty. Zanadu and Zissou are making all the media right now."

"Who?"

"Babies nine and ten."

Zorah Harding. An inspiration to us all . . .

"No Zen?"

I thought for sure that Zen would be used for one of her latest deliveries. All Zorah's deliveries start with *Z*: Zahara, Zoe, Zachary, Zayd, Zsa Zsa, Zeus, Zelda, Zane . . .

He holds up two sets of crossed fingers. "Number eleven!"

With leaden feet, I trudge up the hill of stairs to the hole at the top of the tree. I squeeze myself through the small opening and plop myself down on a pillow. The tree house is meant for toddlers, not teenagers, so we can't both sit inside without part of me touching part of him. I hunch and scrunch myself in such a way that only the soles of our sneakered feet make contact.

"So," Zen says.

"So," I say.

"How's Shoko?"

It's such a simple question. And yet it was one that no one at the birth center seemed to trouble themselves with. My eyes start to water, and not because of Dr. Seuss.

"She'll be out of the hospital in a day or two and go on with her life as if nothing ever happened," I say. "As if she almost didn't die . . ."

And that's when I totally lose it.

I'm sobbing because Shoko almost lost her life and because Malia lost her mind. I'm sobbing for Zorah, who's already given a thumbs-up for her eleventh delivery and little Freya, who aspires to be just like her. I'm weeping for bald and cranky Celine Lichtblau and also for glossy-haired and glowing Ventura Vida, even though I still for seriously hate her and her adorable six-month bump, and for all the other pregging Pro/Ammers and the Cheerclones who'll try again with the Ballers at the next masSEX party and all girls everywhere who are valued far more for what's between their legs than what's between their ears.

286

I'm crying hardest of all for my twin.

My sister.

Pregging with a stranger is degrading enough. But how would I feel if I were forced to *marry* someone I barely know, let alone love? Is it any wonder that she ran off with Jondoe?

Zen strokes my hair.

And now I'm crying for him too.

Because when he's holding me like this, letting me wipe my tears, my snot, and slobber all over his sleeve, size doesn't matter. Forget insufficient verticality. To me, my best friend is bigger and stronger and more capable than any cock jockey on the market. I'm feeling closer to him that I ever have.

"Melody?"

I feel each syllable, his chest buzzing against mine. I can't seem to catch my breath.

"When you said what you said about you and Jondoe, I got jealous."

I want to ask, *As jealous as I get whenever I hear rumors about you taking up with another everythingbut?* But I can't.

Instead, I ask, "Why? You knew I was making it up."

"I know," he says, "But . . ."

"What?"

He loosens his grip on me just enough to reach into his knapsack.

"I have something I want to show you," Zen says.

How many times have I heard Zen say this before

producing an impossible-to-find something or other—World Cup tickets, limited-edition couture denim in my size, whatever—that wasn't impossible for him to find at all. Something he had access to that no one else did.

"Something . . ." He pokes his head out the hole in the tree, surveys the library, then pops his head back in. *"Illegal."*

This isn't unusual. Zen has made many friends by distributing all sorts of contraband MiPlay games from Russia.

"What is it?" I ask, playing along, my voice dropping to a whisper.

Zen reaches deep into his bag and pulls out a tiny lockbox that fits into the palm of his hand. He taps the code and it springs open to reveal a small, square piece of foil.

I don't know what it is, but that's not unusual either. Zen answers before I even ask.

"It's a condom."

harmony
melody

AS HEART- AND STOMACH-WRENCHING AS JONDOE'S CONFESSIONS
are to hear, I can't stop myself from listening.

"Now, about your career," Lib says. "I've got some
media for you."

"Have I gone down in the polls?" Jondoe asks, a note
of panic in his voice.

"Just watch."

Then I hear Melody's voice.

*"Jondoe and I had un-preggy sex. For pleasure. Because we
are in loooooove."*

Oh my grace! Melody and Jondoe?! Did what *we* did?!

"Yes! With CONDOMS!"

"She's LYING! That's SLANDER!" Jondoe splutters.
"I mean. That could kill my career. . . ."

"You're lucky Zorah Harding pushed out numbers nine and ten fifteen minutes ago," Lib says. "Otherwise, Melody going all LOVEMAKEY would be the number one clip on the MiNet. As it is, it's only trending in the top twenty. But don't think that won't do major damage to your man brand. . . ."

There's a pause.

"What are we going to do about this?" Jondoe asks in an uncertain voice.

"I was WAITING for you to ask me that!" Lib claps his hands and lets loose a barky guffaw. "Do you think I would come here without a PLAN?"

Jondoe mumbles incoherently.

"I EXIST for this pregg, Jondoe. I LIVE and I DIE for this pregg. . . ."

I didn't like his messianic talk before, and I certainly don't like it now that he's talking about my baby!

"The way I see it, there are two options," Lib says. "Option number one: We tell the Jaydens the truth, that you bumped with the wrong twin but explain that it hardly makes a difference because Melody and Harmony are the same exact girl who'd make the same exact preggs with you."

No, we're not! And, no, we would not.

"But isn't that a breach of contract?" Jondoe asks.

"No," Lib says. "That's the beauty of it. Because as soon as I found out that Melody had a twin, I wrote a twin proxy pregging clause in the contract that was so brilliantly obscured by legal-sounding bullshit that the Jaydens didn't even notice it was in there. But that might not stop them from suing me for fraud. If they sued, they would lose. But the attorneys' fees would eat up all my profits, and quite frankly I don't feel like going through all the mutherhumping hassle."

"So what's the second option?" Jondoe asks calmly.

"Option number two: We convince the one upstairs . . ."

"Harmony," Jondoe says.

"WHATEVER her name is. We'll have her pretend she's Melody for the duration of the pregnancy. We can send her away, somewhere far and safe. We can say that she's got some high-risk condition and needs bed rest and . . ."

No. I will *not* be treated like property! Not here! Not in Goodside! Not anywhere, ever again!

"We can send the real Melody away somewhere too," Lib continues. "She likes role-playing. Maybe she'd have fun pretending to be her Goodside sister for nine months."

Oh, no. I cannot—I will not—let them do this to Melody. Not when this mess is all my fault.

I've got a new mission now.

I gather up my clothes off the floor and get dressed as quickly and quietly as possible.

"If I bump Melody as planned," Jondoe says slowly, "can't we just let Harmony go back to Goodside and leave her out of this whole mess?"

I don't need to hear any more to know that I've got to

get out of this house. And fast.

"How do you expect her to keep quiet with no incentives to do so?" Lib asks. "If she pretends to be Melody, she will—thanks to that twin proxy pregging clause that I so cleverly inserted into the contract—be entitled to all the financial rewards that would have been earned by her sister."

Fortunately for me, I've got practice in making hasty escapes.

"I didn't have to write it that way, you know. I could have humped her out of all the money, especially when she's probably just gonna go and tithe it to her Church or whatever. But I didn't. And that"—Lib pauses and takes a deep, loud breath—"is why I am a great man."

I open the window and the screen. I get a firm grip of the frame, then swing my body out and down into a vertical hang. There's a clear ten-foot drop between the soles of my sneakers and the ground, and I land gracefully on two feet. I've barely touched down before I take off in a full sprint down the block. This is all a lot easier to do when one is not wearing an ankle-length engagement gown and veil, although without such concealment I'll be easily discovered. Without breaking my stride, I reach into my back pocket and pull out the Lost-and-Found card Zen gave me at the Mallplex.

How could he have known I'd find myself in such a state of emergency?

I fingerswipe the card and pray Zen will make good

on his promise. I pray that he will find me.

Until then, I run and keep on running, trying to put as much distance between me and Lib as possible before he realizes that I—that *we*, this baby and me—are missing.

Even though I'm hurt, betrayed, and have been played for a fool, I regret not being able to give Jondoe a proper goodbye. Maybe it's because I know it's not really a good-bye. He's a part of me forever now, a sacrament that can't be taken back.

Even if it wasn't intended to be mine.

melody
harmony

"A CONDOM!" I SHRIEK, MY VOICE ECHOING AROUND THE ROOM.

Zen clamps his hand over my mouth. "Are you trying to get me arrested?"

"Where did you get that thing?" I mumble into his palm.

"Let's just say that it's an antique," he says, holding it up for me to see the expiration date: MARCH 2025. "The last batch before the ban." He regards it with a look of awe. "It should really be in a museum."

"I didn't think it would look like *that*," I say. "How are you supposed to put *that* on your . . ."

He points helpfully to his crotch. *"This?"*

Even in crisis, Zen can't help but perv for a laugh. Only I'm too tired to laugh.

"Um, yeah."

He looks at the small, square piece of foil, then me.

"The rubber is *inside* the wrapper."

"Oh." He didn't say it in a snarky way, but I feel my face flush with dumb embarrassment nonetheless. I pick it up gingerly by its corner and examine it closely.

"Where did you even get that thing?" Even for Zen, this is quite a coup.

He closes his eyes, inhales deeply.

"How isn't important. It's the why that's important."

"Go on."

"You've noticed that I haven't been around as much lately."

I pinch my lips to stop myself from saying something judgy.

"I wanted you to think that I was cramming for my IAMs, or everythingbutting with random Cheerclones. . . ."

I sit up in the pillows. "You weren't?"

He tugs on his hair. "Most of the time, no."

Of course, the hysterical girl in me is, like, *But that means some of the time, yes.*

"The truth is," he says, nervously running his thumb along his lips, "I just couldn't do it anymore."

"Do what?"

I can't take my eyes off his thumb. His lips.

"I couldn't be so close to you all the time and not . . ."

He presses the thumb into his lips, as if to stop himself from saying the unsayable. Then he reaches across the

295

inches between us and now that same thumb is delicately tracing the outline of my own mouth and I'm afraid to even breathe.

"I . . ."

He stops himself again. The dimples vanish. Gone is the boyish exuberance that wins everyone over. I know Zen's face so well, and yet I've never, in all our years of friendship, seen this expression before. He is transformed and I am transfixed by the way he's looking at me right now, with a mix of longing and hope and . . . fear.

"You *what*?" I'm surprised by my own desperate need to hear what comes next.

But just like that, he withdraws his touch. His eyes go blank for a second before he starts winking and blinking. It's too late. Zen's already caught up in someone else's drama. In two seconds he'll take off to tackle someone else's problem. Typical, only this time, I'm furious. What could possibly be more important than this?

"How are you even on the MiNet?" I mutter. "This whole place is blinded. . . ."

He pauses long enough to raise an eyebrow.

"Right, right," I say. "Their MiNet blind is an insult to hackers everywhere."

After a few more seconds he shuts his eyes with a sense of finality.

"So who needs saving now?" I snap.

He slowly opens his eyes and says simply:

"Your sister."

harmony
melody

I DON'T KNOW HOW LONG I'VE BEEN RUNNING, DARTING DOWN empty side streets and avoiding busy roads, hoping that Zen will reach me before Lib does.

I have to protect myself. I have to protect this baby.

I've found myself on a gravel path cutting through a short stretch of woods. It opens up to a parking lot that abuts a rectangle of red and white grass. A gaming field, obviously, but for what sport I don't know. I hear commotion on the other side of a muddy hill, almost as if all the sheep and cows, goats and horses had been set free simultaneously. I crest a small incline and see that there *are* animals running wild, but of the human variety.

Hundreds, maybe thousands of students are swarming the squat but sprawling brick building. Boys and girls dozing on benches and bounding across car hoods. Boys and girls bouncing on the grass and sulking curbside. Boys and girls, still and silent amid the chaos. More boys and girls and boys and girls and boys and girls than I've ever seen together before in my entire life.

Like everyone in my settlement, I was homeschooled with my housesisters until the Blooming. I've never seen a real school like this before, the kind Melody attends. I want to be normal like them. I want to lose myself in that crowd. But then I remember: I'm not anonymous anymore. I quake at the memory of the riot that broke out at the U.S. Buff-A. If this crowd of thousands found out that I was here . . . Oh my grace. They'd string me up for sure.

I'm starting to worry for my safety when I spot a car approaching the parking lot. The window rolls down and I see . . .

Zen!

The car stops a few feet away from me and I run to greet it. Zen gets out on the driver's side . . . and my sister gets out on the other.

My sister!

I have never, not ever, been happier to see two people in my entire life.

And before I even know it, I'm hugging them and they're hugging me and I'm not lost anymore.

I'm found.

"Thank you, God," I say.

melody
harmony

HARMONY IS BEYOND EMOTIONAL.

She's laughing and crying and having a hard time staying on her feet. Zen and I walk her all wobbly-legged over to a patch of grass and sit her down. Zen respects our privacy and returns to the car. I settle down beside her.

I keep hoping a psychic twin connection will kick in, so each of us would instantly and intuitively know and understand what the other is thinking and feeling. We could just look at each other and be, like, "Ohhhh, okaaay. I get it," and be done with it. But without the benefit of a monozygotic mindbond, the only way we're going to work through our issues is to talk about them. I put in some practice with Ram, but I'm not so good with feelings. Where to begin?

Harmony decides for me.

"I'm so sorry," she says, fresh tears still falling. "I hope you can forgive me."

"I already have." I mean it.

"For *everything*," she says, sniffling. "For . . ." She buries her face in her hands, unable to catalog her mistakes out loud. Which is fine by me because the less I hear about her and Jondoe, the better.

"I know. I forgive you. For *everything*."

Harmony exhales with a shudder. I put an arm around her shoulder to comfort her.

"It's not my forgiveness you need to ask for," I say. "But Ram's . . ."

Harmony startles. "You know about Ram?"

"He came to find you," I reply. "He's a mess without you."

Harmony sighs heavily.

"I understand that you bolted on your honeymoon because you don't love Ram," I say. "But what I don't get is why you were trying to get me to come back with you."

"I *thought* I wanted you to return with me," she says, keeping her eyes on the ground. "Goodside is all I know. As much as I couldn't see myself living there for the rest of my life, I couldn't imagine living anywhere else either. I thought that if we made our own household together, I would feel less alone. I could repent and stay married to Ram, even if he could never love me in that way. . . ."

She doesn't give me time to ask what she means by this. Is Ram in love with someone else?

"I now know how unrealistic it was for me to think you'd join the Church with me," she says matter-of-factly. "It's the only way I've been brought up to be and believe and *I* can't make the commitment myself!" She looks up at me now. "Does that make any sense?"

Yes.

Yes, it does.

"I don't want to be a Surrogette." It's a relief to finally say this out loud for the first time. "I never got to make that choice, and neither did you. Our parents chose for us."

Our eyes meet in commiseration, but I don't turn away. Harmony looks just as intently at me and we don't break the gaze, not even when our shared stare approaches awkwardness. Then a strange sensation comes over me. I don't know how to describe it really, but in this moment, I feel like I'm discovering part of myself through her, and she through me. Something lost, now found.

All at once, we ask the same question at the same time. "What now?"

It's not funny. Not in the least. And yet, for some inexplicable reason, we both giggle, then laugh, then all-out snort and roll on the grass.

When we finally calm down, I mouth the words to help me. Help *us*.

We are smart.

We are stunning.
We are strong.
We are everything we need to be.
I just hope it's enough.

harmony
melody

I LOOK OUT THE WINDOW, THE SCENERY WHIZZING BY TOO quickly to make sense of anything I'm seeing. None of us speak, though Melody's lips are moving. She seems to be praying, even though she's not the praying kind. I want to follow her example but all the verses ring hollow in my heart. And my own prayers in my own words—*please, Lord, let Jondoe come back for me, please*—rival my little house-sisters' pleas in their petty selfishness. I've given God enough hassle already.

Then, without any obvious provocation or warning, Zen taps the steering wheel with his palm to get my attention.

"You're not the only Church girl who has doubts."

A flinty flicker of hope sparks in my chest.

"I'm *not*?"

I can tell that this remark has taken Melody by surprise.

"How do you know?" she asks.

"I *know*," he says resolutely. "There are girls like you in every settlement in the tristate! It's hard for you to wrap your head around, but you can turn away from the Church Orders without turning away from faith."

"I *can*?"

"You can," Zen says, with a pointed look in Melody's direction that implies that there's far more than what he's actually saying. "You're not a blind believer, Harmony; otherwise you would've married that first guy when you were thirteen. You're a thinker. And thinking and following the Church Orders is like trying to take a sip from a shaken-up can of Coke '99."

He's right.

"I was tired of the Church always telling me *what* to believe without explaining why."

Melody finishes my thoughts for me. "But you can't get any answers if you don't ask any questions."

Zen nods appreciatively. He locks eyes with me in the rearview. "You have *choices*, Harmony."

"You do," Melody concurs. "We both do."

I suddenly understand what Melody and Zen are offering me.

They want to help me take permanent leave of Goodside.

Who would miss me if I never came back? Ma? She

already said goodbye—twice—when she tried to marry me off—twice—to someone I didn't—I don't—love. And there are my housesisters, more compliant than I will ever be, who will—who surely already have—taken my place in service of the Church community. My chores have not gone uncompleted in my absence, that's for sure.

The spread of the Virus all around the world has given Church elders good reason to put even stricter prohibitions on our contact with the outside world. By forbidding us to go beyond the gates for all but missionary or agricultural business, we're quarantined from contagions that cause sickness in the body *and* soul. I knew when I left Ram that the red dress—my punishment for going Wayward—would await my return. I hoped that the Council would go easier on me if I saved Melody's soul; a short-term shunning was a small price to pay for her salvation after all. I should have realized much sooner that Melody would never trade her world for mine. I see that now, and my naïveté almost makes me want to cry.

Did I *really* come here to bring Melody to Goodside?

Or did I come here to bring out the Otherside in me?

"We're here," Zen says as he pulls into and up the gravel driveway. "Melody's going to drop me off at school to do some damage control, but she'll be back soon to help you sort this all out. Won't you, Mel?"

"Of course I will," she says. "Ram's waiting for you."

As I get out and take the first uneasy steps toward the house, Melody sticks her head out the car window and gives me a thumbs-up.

"You can do this, sister!"

Sister! Her acceptance uplifts me. I feel as free as the veil that caught the wind and flew away. . . .

I dream of a life where girls don't hide behind veils. And they can dress as they want to and cut their hair or keep it long if that's what they like. And they can study the Bible, really study it by asking questions and having them answered, and also read other, unbiblical books too. Where red is the color of strawberries, cardinals, and morning glories, not shame, shunning, and sin.

A life where girls are free to fall in love . . .

Even if that love proves to be something else entirely.

I want all these things, not just for me, but for the baby growing inside me.

melody
harmony

ZEN INSISTS THAT SCHOOL IS THE BEST PLACE FOR HIM TO do damage control. Apparently Ventura Vida is making major media by spilling all the insidery gossip about me that only a best friend like her would know. But I couldn't care less about her or my image right now. All I can think about is Harmony.

"You think we can help her?"

"I hope so," he says. "Her situation is . . ."

I finish for him. "Complicated."

"To say the least," he says. "But she'll have options out here that she wouldn't have if she went back to Goodside."

And for the first time since I met her, I'm awed by Harmony's bravery. She's rejecting the only life she's ever known in the hopes of building a better future for herself. I'm proud to call her my sister. I can't wait to tell her so.

"You have options too, Mel," Zen says. "You never wanted to be a Surrogette and now, because of Harmony, you may not have to."

"What do you mean?"

"Don't be surprised if she offers to make the delivery to the Jaydens for you," he says frankly.

"I would never ask her to do that!"

"She might do it as a form of penance," he says. "Church guilt runs deep."

I shake my head firmly. "No way."

Mark my words: If it were up to me, no girl would ever sign on to be a Surrogette again.

We pull up in front of the school.

"I'll stick with what Jondoe's Reps are spinning," he says. "That yours is a professional working relationship and you never, ever had lovemakey sex."

I really don't care what anyone thinks about me and Jondoe anymore. Now that I know that there's hope for Harmony, there's only one unresolved issue that needs resolving and it's between me and Zen.

" . . . I'll say you were fotobombed and—"

"Zen?"

I have his undivided attention. "Yes?"

"That Tocin you gave Ram last night," I say. "It was for me."

His mouth falls open.

"You were going to dose me," I say quickly. "Then talk me into using the, um . . . condom. With you."

He jumps up in his seat and smacks his head on the car roof.

"No! I'd—never! No!"

"It's okay. I'm not mad," I insist. "I mean, it was a compromise, right? We could make good on our pact, without jeopardizing my contract with the Jaydens."

Zen is shaking his head, both hands pulling at the hair right above his ears.

"I'd never try to trick you into doing anything like that. With me. Never."

I'm trying not to let this hurt my feelings. "Then who was it for?"

"Me . . ."

His voice trails off and his eyes keep flitting away from mine. It's not that he's on the MiNet. He just can't bring himself to look at me. And I can't bring myself to ask him to.

"You've never been anything but up front about where you stand, Mel. Your contract has always come first. I'm just an optimistic idiot for letting myself believe otherwise. I guess it wasn't until after I confronted you at the Mallplex the other day that I finally said, 'Fuck it.' Literally. Fuck. It. I decided I'd get dosed enough to do it with one of the Cheerclones. It didn't matter which one because none of them were you."

He laughs in a hollow way that makes my chest ache.

"That's when I finally let go of the dream that *my* first time," he says, "would be *our* first time."

harmony
melody

I'VE MEMORIZED PLENTY OF VERSES, BUT PRAYING ON THEM hasn't brought me any closer to understanding what they really mean. Knowing the words doesn't equal knowing the *Word*. When it comes to the Scripture, I'm as superficial as my little housesisters. Maybe I should go back to the basics, the first prayer I ever memorized.

"Forgive us our trespasses as we forgive those who trespass against us," I say to myself, hoping it's not an insult to skip ahead to the part I really need right now. "Lead us not into temptation and deliver us from evil. . . ."

I'm standing in the spot where Jondoe once stood. My finger touches the buzzer Jondoe's finger once pressed. The same finger that traced the curve of my hips . . .

The door opens.

"HARMONY!"

And in an instant I am swept up in an all-encompassing crush of grass and manure, sweat and oatmeal soap.

"Oh, Harmony."

Oh, Ram.

The only person in Goodside who is more lost than I am.

melody
harmony

ZEN IS STRUGGLING. I HAVE NEVER, EVER SEEN HIM AT SUCH A loss for words.

"You have to understand, Mel. You're the only girl I've ever wanted to be with."

"In that way?" I ask.

"In *every* way."

I do understand. More than he can possibly know.

But I can't . . .

Can I?

After sitting in silence for more than a minute, waiting for me to respond to his confession, Zen finally opens his mouth.

"Well." Pause. "I guess I better get." Pause. "Going."

He gets out of the car swiftly, but hesitates before

taking the front steps leading up to the school. I watch him through the window, and something—a biological drive, a human instinct, an evolutionary pull that I'm powerless to resist—takes over. Head to toe. Limb to limb. Top to bottom. Inside and out.

"Wait!"

He runs back over to the car and crouches down in front of the window so my mouth is just inches from his. "What?" he asks.

"Nez."

He slowly breaks into a smile.

"Lem."

And before I can stop myself, I cradle his cheeks in my hands, pull him close, part my lips, and . . .

My first kiss.

Ours.

All of us.

All of our ancestors, and all of our descendants, are coming together to celebrate this kiss, to clap and fist-pump and foot-stomp and shout out loud to the universe YES! YES! A million billion years of YESSSS!

We break apart, stunned and breathless.

And for a moment, I'm afraid that Zen will launch into a quikiwiki spiel about how kissing is a sort of evolutionary taste test, that healthier offspring are produced by part-ners with different immune proteins, and those differences can be detected in the sloppy swap of genetic information encoded in our spit.

But he doesn't say any such thing. Instead, I find out what he started to say in the tree house.

"I love you."

And then he breaks into the most deranged grin I've ever seen on anyone, anywhere, except maybe my own crazyface in the rearview mirror.

harmony
melody

WHEN I LAY DOWN WITH JONDOE, HE PROMISED TO SHOW ME the Truth.

I just wish it hadn't taken me until right now to see it clearly.

"Ram . . ." I begin. "I'm . . ."

"I forgive you," Ram says automatically.

I need to be punished. How can I expect to be punished by a sweet soul whose transgressions are far worse than my own?

"When Melody found out I was with—" My throat closes on his name.

"With *him*?" Ram asks.

I nod. "How did she react?"

Like a little kid avoiding trouble, Ram looks every-where—his feet, the ceiling, out the window, down the hall—but at me.

"What did she say, Ram? I have to know."

He speaks quickly, hoping to get this unpleasantness over with. I brace myself for the worst.

"She said she wished you had never come into her life." He gulps down more air. "She wished you had never been born."

It's a relief, really, to hear what I have most feared.

I don't deserve Melody's forgiveness.

I don't deserve Zen's help.

I don't deserve Jondoe's love.

This is my punishment.

I take a breath and force a smile to my face. "I have blessed news, Ram."

"What?" His eyes are shiny with tears.

I swallow hard and pat my belly.

"We're having a baby."

He blinks.

"But . . . I didn't . . ."

There had always been rumors about Ram being of an unmentionable kind. That despite his brawn, he was soft. More interested in watching the boys than the girls.

"We didn't . . ."

That's why the Church Council chose him for me. Better to put the two unteachable spirits together than admit defeat and cast us off entirely.

"Did we?"

I hold my hand up to stop his stammering. Ram needs me far more than I need him. He can't go back to Good-side without me. And I can't stay in Otherside with him. It wouldn't be fair, not when I know that Jondoe is out here too. The temptation to be unfaithful—in my heart if not in action—would be too great.

"Do you want to start over?"

As the first tear falls down his face and splashes into his steepled hands, I know his answer.

"Yes."

"Me too."

It's finally time for *me* to assert *my* spiritual leadership. One of us has to.

"Let's go back home and have this baby," I say. "Together."

melody
harmony

WITH ZEN'S KISS STILL FRESH ON MY LIPS, I'M READY TO FACE anything.

"Hello?" I call out as I open the front door.

Before the vowel bounces its echo off the walls, I know my house is empty. I know that Ram has gone. And with a sudden spine-tingling chill, I know something else.

Harmony is gone too.

I walk, zombielike, to the common room, where there's a note lying on top of the ergomatic couch cushions still dented by Ram's bulk. It's written on a page torn out of a Bible. Just the title page, nothing more, no verses offering clues to her state of mind when she wrote two words in a handwriting that I could easily mistake for my own:

Forgive me.

But I *have* forgiven her! Why didn't she believe me?

It's true that Harmony shouldn't have gone off with Jondoe like that. But she's still my sister, maybe the only blood relation I will ever know. She must still think I hate her as deeply as I thought I did, that is, before I realized that spermjacking Jondoe was the best thing that ever could have happened to me.

To us.

Harmony and Ram couldn't have gotten very far on foot, so I immediately take off after her. I fling open the front door, and facesmash right into a perfect set of pectorals.

"It's me!" Jondoe announces unnecessarily.

I must say that crashing into the hottest RePro on the MiNet is not nearly as exciting as I thought it would be. Not now, after everything that has happened. He looks for seriously amped for a second before leaning in to get a good look at my freckleless nose. His whole body sags when he realizes that I'm not the twin he was hoping for.

"You're Melody," he says flatly. "The one who's trying to ruin me."

"I am," I reply. "But I'm not." I try to push past him, but he slings his arm across the door to stop me.

"CONDOMS?!" His eyes bug out. It's quite comical, really. I could make a lot of money selling a foto of him looking goofy like that.

"I was only trying to get you two out of hiding," I reply. "And it worked, didn't it? You're here."

He cranes his neck to stalk over my shoulder. "Where's Harmony?"

"She's not here," I say. "She just took off, and I was on my way after her."

"She ran off on you too?" he says. "She climbed out my window! My *window*!"

He's almost too impressed by her escape act to be upset by it. Almost. I realize I have no idea what really happened between these two. As queasy as I am to hear the details, I have to ask.

"Why did she go out the window?"

"She must have overheard me bullshitting your agent."

Lib found her before I did, as I knew he would. But I can't worry about Lib right now.

"About what?"

"About tricking her into believing that I have God," he says, visibly agitated. "The thing is, I was telling her the truth! Well, at first I was scamming. But then, I don't know, something came over me and I wasn't faking it anymore. It's like I really felt God laying love for her in my heart, but I couldn't let Lib know that!"

As much as I don't want to know, I have to know.

"So you two . . ."

I search for the most tactful way to say what I want to say, and abandoning that, find myself mimicking Zen's finger-in-the-hole gesture.

Jondoe flashes his famous trillion-dollar smile. "Did we *ever.*"

Gaaaah.

When I've recovered from gagging, I ask, "Do you think you bumped?"

The smile disappears. A vein pops out of his forehead.

"What's it with everyone questioning my spermhood? I don't turn eighteen for another six months!"

I burst out laughing. I can't believe this icon of maleness is acting so wanky. Shoko would never believe it.

"Lib wants to cut you out of the deal, you know," Jondoe warns. "He thinks he can make a side deal with the Jaydens for Harmony's delivery."

"Yeah, I know," I say. "And I don't care."

"You don't *care?*" Jondoe double-takes.

"There's not enough money in the world for me to bump with you."

I can't believe I've just said this to the world-famous cock jockey. I expect him to be offended. But instead he says, "I know exactly what you mean."

He closes his eyes and rests his head on the doorframe. I seize this opportunity to lean in and take a quick whiff. You know. For Shoko. I can now confirm that Jondoe smells like every other teenage boy who hopes to jack his swagger by dousing themselves in bottle after bottle of Jondoe: the Fragrance.

"When I first got into the business, my agent warned me against falling for a girl who would make me want to give it all up," he says. "A girl who could see the real me, not just what's in my file."

He looks up in agony. An *alluring* agony.

"Your sister is that girl," he says. "And you've got to help me find her."

Is Jondoe really smitten with Harmony? Or is he plotting with Lib? I don't know what to believe.

"Everything changed when I met your sister," Jondoe says. "It's like I didn't even know myself until she came into my life."

I smile, thinking that Harmony did the same thing for me.

"Please help me find her," he says quietly. "Please."

I want to believe that Jondoe's being sincere. But I'm hesitant to buy into his sad-eyed, pouty-lipped sexy act. Did Harmony find him irresistible because she didn't know any better? Or because he really showed her part of himself that he'd never revealed before? I guess there's only one way of finding out.

"Maybe," I suggest, "we can all help each other."

And that's when the hottest RePro on the MiNet pulls me into those perfect pecs of his and squeezes me in gratitude.

I'm sixteen. I'm not pregnant.

But at this very moment, I feel like the most important person on the planet.

Acknowledgements

MANY THANKS GO OUT TO:

Alessandra Balzer, whose no-nonsense editorial wisdom saved me—and this book. Period. And Donna Bray and everyone else at this fantastic imprint and HarperCollins at large for helping me make my debut as an "official" YA author.

Heather Schroder at ICM, whose eye-popping response to my hypothetical ("What if only teenagers could get pregnant?") began what I hope to be a long and rewarding relationship. And Josie Freedman, also at ICM, for trying to introduce my characters to a whole new audience on screen.

Rachel Cohn, for convincing me that I was up to the challenge, especially at the overwhelming start.

CJM, whose early insight inspired me so much more than he will ever give himself credit for.

And CJM, for always asking, "How was your day today?" and reminding me that even a bad day of writing is better than not writing at all.

TURN THE PAGE FOR A SNEAK PEEK AT

thumped

harmony
melody

I FACE MY REFLECTION, AN ENGORGED DISTORTION I BARELY
recognize anymore.

"I'll do it this time," I say to the mirror.

I mean it too. I'm alone here in my bedroom. The
blades are sharp enough and there's no one here to stop me
but myself.

Until they come for me.

"Harmony!" Ma calls from down the hall. "You're
missing your own nesting party!"

My housesisters and I have been preparing for this party
for eight and a half months. Every morning I've joined
Katie, Emily, and Laura in their household for prayer and
purposefulness. Now we're stocking the nursery's shelves
with the cloth diapers, knitted booties, and cotton jumpers

we have to show for our collective efforts.

All four of us received the sacrament of marriage on the same day in a group ceremony. We're all with child, but I'm the furthest along and the only one carrying twins. I'm also three years older than they are, so that often makes me feel more like a housemother than a housesister to them. For these reasons, they say, the Church Council voted to give Ram and me our own house to keep, the only couple in the settlement that doesn't have to share with three other families.

There's a gentle knock on the door as it opens. I quickly conceal the shears in my apron pocket.

"May I come in?" Ma asks as she pokes her head in the room. "Are you still woozy?"

I'd felt fine all morning until Ma had presented me with two exquisite hand-stitched quilts in the traditional pattern of interlocking hearts and halos.

"May you be as blessed as I have been," Ma had said as she handed over her gift, a gesture that symbolized the bestowment of motherhood—of womanhood—from one generation to the next.

At that moment, I had to leave the nursery. I couldn't breathe in that room. It felt like four tiny feet were stomping my windpipe when in fact the twins hadn't moved inside me at all.

Now Ma reaches up to press her palm against my sweaty forehead. Without thinking, I clutch my hand against hers and am somewhat surprised by how cool her skin feels under mine. She inhales sharply, so I know that she's startled by the gesture too. I'm relieved when she doesn't resist because I can count on our two joined hands how many times in my sixteen-almost-seventeen years we've had a moment alone together like this. Our household never had fewer than a dozen children at one time to care for, so Ma always had to be efficient with her time and attention. Ma is raising eight of the neediest children in the settlement right now, all of whom are under the age of five. Surely there are infants crying in their bassinets, waiting to be soothed. Babies she didn't give birth to—like me—but were placed by the Church Council to be raised by her righteous example.

When she retracts her hand, mine falls away and hangs limply at my side.

"Would it help to know that I felt overwhelmed during my first pregnancy?" she asks. "I wasn't that much older than you are now."

Before the Virus, women could wait until they turned eighteen to get married and have babies. Now, for all but a very few of us around the world, within a year or two of that birthday marks the end of our child-bearing years. At sixteen-almost-seventeen, I'm considered a very late bloomer.

"Put all your faith in God. He will never give you anything more than you can handle."

Ma stands up and brushes the invisible dust off her apron as if the matter of my overwhelming maternity is all settled. She is nothing if not practical. When your whole life has been devoted to taking care of others, you have to be. Small and stout with curly black hair and brown eyes, Ma has never looked anything like me. But for some reason those physical differences are all I can see right now.

"Take a few moments to pray on it before rejoining us." She smiles benignly, then slips out the door.

Ma means well. She always does. But I feel like I've already been dealt more than I can handle. I've seen that formerly empty room for what it was destined to be all along: a nursery. Two quartersawn oak cribs, one against each wall. A changing table stacked with cloth diapers. A braided rug on the floor in soft shades of yellow and green. A glider and ottoman near the window. But try as I might, I can't envision the babies sleeping in their cribs. Being changed out of a soiled diaper. Or rolling happily on the rug. And it is all but impossible to picture myself rocking back in forth in the glider, nursing a ravenous baby on each breast. I know now, beyond a shadow of a doubt, that unlike the three other girls in the room with Ma, I will never live up to her example.

A riot breaks out in my belly. The thrashing of four tiny feet, the pounding of four tiny fists. The twins are awake.

"Are you two trying to stop me?" I whisper. "Or do you want me to go through with it?"

Another round of kicking and punching.

I choose to interpret this as a sign of encouragement.

After eight and a half months, I'm convinced the twins feel as trapped as I do. I take the shears out of my pocket and return my attention to the mirror with a renewed sense of purpose. I grip the handle, all ready to go through with my plan, when I'm stopped by the sound of my name once more.

"Harmony!"

Only this time, it's not Ma. And it's not coming from down the hall.

"It's me . . ."

It's *him*.

"Please pick up . . ."

Calling to me from the MiVu screen.

Oh my Grace. I've blinded his profile countless times, but he keeps coming back.

"Harmony . . ."

I don't want to look at his face. I draw upon every last ounce of strength I have left not to look. . . .

But I can't help myself. And there he is, larger than life on the screen, looking every bit as tortured and handsome as he did the last time he tried to contact me a few weeks ago.

Jondoe. Or *Gabriel*, as he should be known.

No, I will only know him as Jondoe.

"You're at thirty-five weeks today, Harmony. I just want to make sure you're okay. . . ."

He looks so sincere. But how can I ever believe someone who gets paid to lie?

5

"Please let me see you . . . I miss your face."

Right now I hold all the power. I can see him. But he can't see me.

And if I have my way, he never will.

I briskly walk over to the MiVu screen and blind his profile again.

melody
harmony

MY TWIN IS EVERYWHERE, AND YET SHE'S NOWHERE TO BE seen.

"She blinded me again," Jondoe says with a sigh, a sigh with 180 pounds of perfectly sculpted musculature behind it. Not that his hot body is doing him a bit of good these days. He's miserable, and it's all because of my sister.

"I'm sorry," I say. "But I told you she would."

Harmony is the most determined person I've ever met. Eight and a half months ago, she made up her mind that returning to Goodside to deliver the twins was the "godly" thing to do. She hasn't wavered in that decision, despite all our repeated attempts to woo her back to this side of the gates. Harmony insists on raising them with Ram, even though there's zero chance that her husband is the true father.

"Do you have any idea how hard it is to be here?" Jondoe asks. "Surrounded by girls who look *exactly* like her?"

The irony is, I'm Harmony's identical twin and I'm not even one of the girls Jondoe is referring to. I scan the rowdy crowd from the safety of the one-way window wall of our second-story VIP room. There are a lot of girls who look just like her at a distance. It's impossible to count just how many dyed blondes are dressed in Conception Couture knockoffs of Harmony's green maternity gown.

Jondoe anxiously chews on his thumbnail. "Is it even safe for her to deliver in Goodside? Do they even have real doctors there?"

"Delivering is what they do best," I say, taking Harmony's word for it because that's all I have. I mean, Goodside midwives must know what they're doing if they routinely deliver babies for teen newlyweds, right?

But before I can say anything else to reassure him, my agent, Lib, comes barreling toward us wearing the latest TEAM HOTTIE T-shirt under the pink and blue flashing lumina jacket that has become his iconic trademark. I hate that shirt. I especially hate that I'm wearing the same exact shirt in size XXXL Maternity.

"Your FANS are ready for YOU! Are YOU ready for THEM?"

"We're ready." I look to Jondoe for confirmation, but he's too distracted to pay me or Lib or this party any mind.

Lib has no time for such self-indulgent melodrama,

unless he's the one being self-indulgently melodramatic. He pokes Jondoe in the ribs.

"Ow!" Jondoe says, rubbing the spot.

"You think you can interrupt your VERY IMPORTANT LIP POUTING long enough to fulfill your contractual obligations?"

Jondoe shrugs.

Lib shoots me a *he's your problem* look, then takes off to welcome the incoming crowd.

As soon as he's out of earshot, Jondoe leans in.

"I can't believe Harmony is really going to stay there with Ram." His voice is on the verge of breaking. "You promised that she'd come around before she delivered."

"I thought she would . . ."

I really did too.

"You told me this was how I could help her," he says bitterly, more to himself than me. "That's the only reason I'm still here . . ."

He silences himself as the room fills with fan clubbers, contest winners, and corporate muckety-mucks, all eager to have their fotos taken with us.

I believe Jondoe has sincere feelings for my sister. I mean, the guy can sell underwear like nobody's business, but that pretty much pushes the limit of his skills as an actor. There's no way that he could have faked the change I've seen in him for the past eight and a half months. I know it has sucked for Jondoe—I can relate all too well with wanting to be with someone you can't have.

9

I bring my lips to his ear.

"She's the reason I'm here too," I say. "And there's still time."

But even as I say these words, I know that with each minute that goes by, they are that much closer to becoming more lies.

Our audience swoons over our whispered sweet nothings, the secrets shared by two gorgeous ReProductive Professionals who have done the unheard of:

We have fallen deeply and lustily in love.

At least that's what we need everyone to believe they're seeing.

harmony
melody

I DID IT! IF I CAN RESIST JONDOE, I CAN DO ANYTHING. I'M flush with a rush of energy like I haven't felt since my second trimester.

With one hand I take hold of my long braid and extend it as far as it will go. With the other hand I open the shears. I place the thick golden plait inside the mouth of the scissors, close my eyes, and . . .

"What in Heaven are you *doing*?"

My husband has a knack for showing up precisely when he's not wanted.

Ram is frozen in the door frame, his whole face etched with concern. I know this gentle giant cares about me, loves me even, just not in the way in he should. And yet, I cared enough about him to come back here because he needed me more than I needed him. It's how my ma raised me, after all, to live in JOY:

Jesus first, Others next, Yourself last.

That's the excuse I use anyway, whenever anyone asks why I gave up on my fresh start in Otherside before it even had a chance to begin. Yet, as far as I know, according to stolen conversations I've had with Melody, there's really only *one* person who asks. But after everything that has happened, I don't think I'll ever be convinced that Jondoe needs me out there nearly as much as Melody says he does, and certainly not more than Ram needs me here. Jondoe has amassed a fortune making fools fall for his untruths. We *both* have, actually. But I won't be *his* fool again.

Or anyone else's.

Ram approaches me slowly, carefully, like I'm a rabid dog or something worth fearing.

"Your ma and your housesisters are waiting for you," he says.

His hand is outstretched, hoping I'll willingly give him the scissors without an argument. Praying that I will, against all odds, act like the subservient wife he's never asked me to be. Instead, I take an even tighter grip on the handles, clamp down firmly one . . . two . . . three times until the braid comes away in my fist!

Ram and I take a moment to marvel at it, as if this length of hair were a rare and dangerous creature I had hunted down and caught with my bare hands.

I'm still staring at my quarry when I hear the high-pitched gasps.

"Oh my Grace!"

Ma tries in vain to block my housesisters from getting a clear look at what I've just done. Hands flutter to mouths, cheeks, and eyes in disbelief.

"The Orders!" my housesisters cry out in unison. "She broke the Orders!"

I lock eyes with the woman who raised me. There's no comfort to be found in her gaze, only sadness. I hope she knows this isn't her fault. Ma treated all her daughters—by birth and by adoption, before me and after—the same. Forty-seven out of forty-eight of the children she raised were receptive to her teachings of the Word. I don't know why I am the exception.

"I'm praying for you," Ma says as she ushers Katie, Emily, and Laura out of the doorway. There's a finality to the way she says it, as if she's brushing me off like so much invisible dust on her apron.

The front door slams and Ram finally speaks. There's a catch in his voice. He's scared. And I am too.

"What *are* you doing, Harmony? What are *we* going to do?"

At eight and a half months along, I don't have much time left for figuring out the answer. I rub the naked nape of my neck and do what I haven't been able to do since I came back all those months ago: Tell the truth.

"I don't know."

Want to find out what happens next?

MEGAN McCAFFERTY

Bestselling author of the Jessica Darling series

thumped

The sequel to BUMPED

The startling sequel to *Bumped*

BALZER + BRAY
An Imprint of HarperCollinsPublishers

www.epicreads.com

JOIN
THE COMMUNITY AT

Epic Reads
Your World. Your Books.

DISCUSS
what's on your reading wish list

FIND
the latest books

CREATE
your own book news and activities to share with friends

ACCESS
exclusive contests and videos

Don't miss out on any upcoming EPIC READS!

Visit the site and browse the categories to find out more.

www.epicreads.com

HARPER TEEN
An Imprint of HarperCollinsPublishers